D0720897

SWAMP ANGEL

Dorothy Langley

SWAMP ANGEL

Academy
Chicago

Academy Chicago
425 N. Michigan Ave.
Chicago, IL 60611
All rights reserved
Printed and bound in the USA
© 1982 by Helen Bugbee

ISBN 0-89733-06-9
ISBN 0-89733-06-7 pbk.

Library of Congress Cataloging in Publication Data

Langley, Dorothy, 1904-1969.
  Swamp angel.

    I. Title.
PS3562.A5116 1982   813'.54   82-18421
ISBN 0-89733-060-9
ISBN 0-89733-061-7 (pbk.)

Introduction

The term "swamp angel," like the better known "hill billy," designates a member of a group of Americans who remained in rural isolation while most of the country became increasingly urban if not always urbane. Both groups were of early American Anglo-Saxon stock, but the swamp people lived in swampy areas which have been undergoing drainage in the last fifty years, while the hills of the hill people remain.

To Americans in 1982, swamp angels may seem like inhabitants of another planet, but back in 1920, when Dorothy Langley encountered them as a young teacher fresh out of high school in the highly civilized small community of Bloomfield, Missouri, they were only 35 miles from home. In 1920, however, Henry Ford's contraption had not yet obliterated distances like 35 miles. Once arrived among her swamp angels, Miss Langley was as isolated as they were from the world she knew. But she was young and her mind and heart and pores were open, so she recognized their humanity as having much in common with her own. Throughout her life she protested the patronizing attitude— or worse—of writers who treated similar people as sub-human freaks.

Miss Langley taught the lower four grades in a two-room school in which her older brother taught the upper four. Most of the children had what then was known as seven-year itch as well as malaria, and when they had a chill, simply put their heads down on their desks until it ended.

With her brother she lived in a shack with a stovepipe chimney and of course without plumbing. She shared the life of the community, assisting at childbirth and laying out the dead and playing the organ at revival meetings, where she developed a lifelong love of the gospel music of which Sir Rowland Hill had commented "Why should the Devil have all the good tunes?"

In "Swamp Angel" Dorothy Langley tells the story of some people who lived in a swamp community similar to the one where she taught. None of the characters is drawn precisely from life, but they are all true to life not only in the swamps of southeast Missouri but wherever people have not been deprived of genuineness, naturalness, and simplicity— in other words, "sophisticated."

It may be difficult for people in a Chicago high-rise or faculty common room to accept their kinship with people who have not developed the defenses against their emotions that constitute sophistication. But the differences are superficial. A revival preacher with a faith as simple as that of Brother Pointer and the people to whom he carried his rousing gospel message did not understand that emotions once aroused can take unintended directions. But neither did the troubled people of Vienna who carried their problems to Sigmund Freud. And who can deny that on every level of society there are relations between husband, wife, and children as traumatic as those between Tim and Bertha Mallory and their son Clarence? The violence is manifested differently, of course. It is camouflaged, "sophisticated." But it is just as murderous, though it murders only spirits. As for the daughter who found no love at home and turned elsewhere for a cheap substitute, the city streets know her by the hundreds. There are no strangers in this novel, just human beings without the disguises with which most of us are familiar. Like the colonel's lady and Judy O'Grady, we're all relatives under the skin, and Dorothy Langley treated her people that way.

Some of the material and some of the characters now presented in "Swamp Angel" were used first in an early version of Dorothy Langley's first published novel, "Wait for Mrs. Willard," but the publishers of that book wanted a conventional happy ending, and Miss Langley deserted her swamp angels to supply it. Though she lived to regret having compromised to get her first novel published, her swamp angels deserved stronger treatment than she had given them as subordinate figures in the earlier book. In "Swamp Angel" Miss Langley more than made up for her early compromise and has given them her full attention in a book of their own.

—**Helen Bugbee**
Chicago, Illinois
July, 1982

I

The woman rode like fury, a column of yellow dust rising behind her and her mare's hooves rattling dully against the dried and rutted mud of the lower swamp trail. She rode without a saddle and not astride. She had magnificent red hair, flung back from a face so white with rage that her deep-set dark eyes in the midst of it were terrifying. The hair was long and heavy and had been rolled into a loose knot at the nape of her neck, but now it was losing its pins and falling down her back.

In spite of the blinding August heat, she wore over her calico house dress a ragged gray woollen sweater. Bent forward against nothing, as though by the mere thrust of her strong shoulders she could push her unseen adversary out of her way, she galloped past house after house after house—shanties they were, most of them, like the one she herself lived in, with leather-hinge doors and chimneys made of stovepipe—looking neither to the right nor to the left.

She knew that women were coming out to stare at her as they always did. "Let 'em," she said to herself. "Makes no differ'nce to me what they think. I don't keer two whoops!"

1

And it was true that she did not care. Who could care for the maundering opinions of these slatternly, stringy-haired, shapeless, snaggle-toothed women whose husbands daily trod them into the ground as though they were beetles? "I don't want no part of 'em," she said.

But there were many things she did want, and she wanted them no less desperately because she would not have been able to say what they actually were. Only one of them was sharp and clear in her mind. It had to do with Tim Mallory.

Tim Mallory was her husband, and she wanted him to die, and he would not. She had been married to him fourteen years; she was now nearly thirty, and her eldest son was thirteen. She had five other children besides.

She hated Tim with a silent, grinding hatred that gave her no rest night or day. She hated his mean stature, his rooster-like strut, his fatuous self-approval and his loud and frequent outbursts of opinion. She hated his senseless cruelty—Tim counted that day lost when he had no child to flog—and his equally senseless fits of amiability, which never lasted long because her contemptuous silence in the face of his blandishments threw him immediately back into a rage. She hated serving him, as her position as his wife and in the community required; she dropped his food in front of him as though she were feeding, against her will, an evil troll out of a fairy tale. She knew that he perceived her loathing of her enforced servitude and gloated upon it, and she hated him for that gloating as for nothing else she had against him.

Her children, all but one, were wholly unlike her, for they had long since been bullied out of any but a reminding resemblance to normal human young. In their father's presence they were meek as rabbits and colorless as rainwater, and in his absence they revenged themselves upon him by attacking one another.

Their mother's attitude toward them was, on the whole, dispassionate. She protected them when she could and stoically endured their punishments when she could not, silently adding each one to her score against her husband.

But they had not much of a hold upon her heart; essentially they were like Tim, and she knew it. "All but one," she said to herself bitterly, "and that one too ornery to live."

She turned the mare, the worst of her fury spent, and started home. A tall old man with white hair and a placid countenance, with eyes of the frosty blue that comes with age, lifted a hand in greeting as she passed him. "Good mornin', Mis' Mallory," he said, and smiled in deprecation of this formal mode of address. "Seems like I can't never rightly recollect your given name in time. It's Berthy, ain't it?"

Mrs. Mallory acknowledged it with the briefest of nods. "Mornin', Brother Pointer," she mumbled grudgingly. She did not want to talk with anybody, least of all a preacher. She dug her heel into the mare's flank. "Git up, Jess!" she cried.

The mare broke into a gallop. The old man would still be standing there, Bertha knew, looking after her. Well, she hadn't wanted to be short with him, but let him leave her alone. Let him take his merciful God to somebody with less on her mind. A different kind of God, she felt, was needed to deal with Tim Mallory.

Arrived at home, she saw her nine-year-old twins, Clovis and Woodrow, playing in the yard with a stray dog. "Woodrow!" she called. "Come open thishere gate."

The little boy came toward her, squinting in the sun. The dog trotted behind him.

Bertha fixed Woodrow with a stern eye. "You and Clovis better git that dog outen the yard before *he* comes in from the field," she said as she rode through the gate. "Unlest you want to git your heads laid wide open and the dog's head too."

"We will," promised Woodrow, hunching up his shoulders in a way he had. "We'll git him out. Cain't we give him somethin' to eat first, Maw—some cornbread or somethin'?"

"I don't keer what you do," said Bertha shortly, "jest so you git him out in time." She dismounted, leaving Jess still bridled in the yard, and strode toward the house in renewed fury—fury directed this time against herself, that she could

not bring herself to name her husband to her children. "He,"
she had called him, and she knew that she could call him
nothing else, either to herself or to them. The words "your
daddy," when occasionally she forced them out for empha-
sis, all but strangled her.

There was a soreness at her heart that she had spoken so
brusquely to Woodrow. But what else, she fiercely defended
herself to herself, could she have done? He had lifted his
shoulders at her in Tim's very way; both he and Clovis had
Tim's causeless swagger. "I can't stand to look at it, that's
all," she muttered as she went into the house.

Why was it, she wondered with a dull pain in her breast,
that she must see her children as they were? Other women
did not. Other women saw no blemish in their children, or if
they did they excused it or were secretly proud of it. But
Bertha saw five of her six children growing up to be spiritual
replicas of Tim Mallory in spite of anything she knew how
to do. In time they would mistreat their own children as he
had mistreated them; in time, each of them would take hold
of the life of some man or some woman as Tim has taken
hold of hers, and slowly, lustfully, luxuriously press it to
nothingness. Most people, Bertha knew, were not so durable
as she.

She saw her other child, Clarence, her eldest and dearest,
almost certainly the victim of his own frustrated passions, so
like her own. Already he was growing sullen and unruly,
and she had more than once seen him look at his father with
the impulse to murder crouching in his eyes. He kept her in
continual terror of what he might one day bring upon himself. Again and again she awakened in the middle of the
night, sweat springing from her upper lip and the palms of
her hands, from a dream that she had seen him glaring
behind bars.

She heard him now in the next room practicing stealthily
on the feeble old violin that had been left behind by a
wandering minstrel. She stepped to the door and looked at
him. "I thought you was supposed to be helpin' him out in
the field," she said.

Clarence did not reply. He was a tall boy, looking rangy and uncompact even when he sat. He had dragged a cane-bottomed chair over to the south window in order to watch, while he played, for a possible surprise appearance of his father. At Bertha's intrusion he lifted his perpetually smouldering dark eyes and flung his head back to get the lank, straggling, ill-cut brown hair off his forehead.

Clarence was not a good-looking boy in any sense of the word. He was not handsome, and he did not look good. A mask of stubbornness and rebellion shut away the identity of his countenance, leaving it as blank as a shuttered window. His one appealing feature, a wide expressive mouth capable of both passion and humor, was set now in a repellent line. He looked at his mother, not with defiance but with the next thing to it; he would be as defiant as she liked, his manner said, if she made it necessary.

"Did he send you in fer somethin'?" Bertha demanded.

"Yeah. Water," Clarence said briefly, and lifted the ragged bow again.

Bertha's quick temper flared. "You want him to wear you out again, Clance?" she snapped, her bosom heaving. "You go git that water and git out there with it right now. First thing you know he'll be in here a-ravin' like a crazy man."

Clarence, with elaborate unconcern, played a meditative note or two. He carefully avoided meeting his mother's eyes.

Bertha dug her nails into her palms. "Clance. Did you hear me?"

"Sure," said Clarence calmly. "I heerd you."

"Then you mind me!" Bertha took three steps forward, snatched the fiddle from his hands and glared at him. "A little more out of you, young man, and I'd break thishere thing into kindlin' wood acrost my knee. You git up from there and go draw that water and git out, do you hear me?"

Clarence rose. "Put that there fiddle down," he commanded. "That there's my fiddle. You put it down."

She held it away from him, and he lunged forward and took it from her. They stood tense, fronting each other, their hands unconsciously clenched in the selfsame way. "I won't hit you," Clarence said at last, thickly. "I wouldn't hurt you. But you let my fiddle alone." He hung the fiddle on its row of nails and looked at her again. "You hear me?" he said, his voice suddenly the rumbling voice of a man. He turned his back on her and left the house.

Bertha took a step or two after him, her punitive impulse blazing in her eyes; but then she stopped, for her head was whirling. Something had leapt at her out of the boy's eyes, something that made her know she could no longer hold him in check. It was Clance and Tim for it now, and the devil take the hindmost.

She drew a long uneven breath and glanced at the sun outside. It was nearly noon, and dinner must soon be on the table. But there was a raging tumult in her blood. Clarence's open defiance, his rearing incipient manhood, had filled her full of restlessness and undefined longing. She laid her hot face for a moment against the window, feeling the cool glass against it; then she realized that she was still wearing the heavy sweater into which she had blindly thrust her arms in her fury of the early morning. She unbuttoned it listlessly, her fingers scarcely aware of buttons or wool. There was a small whorled mirror over the unpainted wooden wash stand at her side, and into this she gazed unseeingly for a moment or two; then, becoming aware of the burning of her eyes and the agitation of her fine deep bosom, she turned from it and set about her work.

She was often hard put to it to find any work to do. The bare little farmhouse was almost ferociously clean, for there were only four rooms and she had few other outlets for her passionate energy. During the early morning hours, today as every day, she had herded her pallid little girls out of her way as she scrubbed and sanded and flung the bedclothing about; she wanted no help from them, although guilt often assailed her at the realization that she was doing nothing to train them for their future destiny as housewives. Opal, the eldest of them, was twelve now and might be expected to marry in three years—four at most. Daisy was seven and the baby, Ardeth, nearly three.

Of all her six children, only Clarence had cost Bertha much in the way of physical anguish. She gave birth easily and scornfully and had always held herself aloof from the gloating reminiscent whines with which the other women of the community celebrated parturition. She helped her neighbors on these occasions, as was expected of her, while their cheerful overalled husbands shot craps or played rummy with friends in an adjoining room. It was a task she hated and one from which she always emerged white with inner conflict. Her sense of the injustice of the situation was maddening, but she knew an unwilling secret envy of the men. They were not expected to take any part in the puling business. The dismal howls from the birth-chamber did not disturb them. "Aw, the ol' lady enjoys it," one of them had said to her, when in her earlier and softer years she had protested; and, although she realized instantly that he was more than half right, the knowledge did little to abate her sense of outrage.

She went now to a strap-hinged cabinet in her shedlike kitchen and took out half a ham, beginning to slice it with clean decisive strokes. Tim would soon be in, wanting his midday meal. She built up the fire in the range, wiping her hot face with her calico apron, and put the ham on to fry in an iron skillet. "Daisy!" she shouted over her shoulder, after another swift reconnaissance of the cabinet, "the eggs is all gone. Go out to the barn and see if you can find some." She took a stack of thick white crockery plates from a shelf, topped them with a clattering pile of bone-handled knives, forks and spoons, and distributed them about the oilcloth-covered table with practised rapidity.

The heat was staggering. On the sunny window sill a heavy fly, torpid and unmoving, lay glistening like a fly of painted lead. She killed it and brushed it out upon the ground, snapping the cheesecloth screen back into place with a bang. For a moment she stood at the window fanning herself.

Daisy came out of the barn with the eggs in her skirt, bits of straw clinging to her legs. "Can I set the table, Maw?" she demanded as she entered. "Here's the eggs. I only found five."

"Them's enough to scramble," Bertha said briefly as she carried them to the kitchen.

Daisy followed. "Can I set the table?" she repeated querulously.

"It's set a'ready. Ain't you got no eyes in your head? And quit that whinin' thataway when you talk." Bertha cracked the eggs over the skillet in rapid succession. "You can go put a clean dress on Ardeth if you got to have somethin' to do."

Daisy's face fell. "Which dress, Maw?"

"Whichever'n you can find. What differ'nce does it make? Where's Opal at?"

Daisy shook her head.

"Well, when you git Ardeth cleaned up, go find her. And call Clovis and Woodrow. Clance will be in with his daddy, I guess. And Daise!" she shouted as the little girl turned away, "you see if the twins has got rid o' that there tramp dog they was playin' with a while ago. If they ain't, you tell 'em to take their foot in their hand and git him out o' here before their daddy comes in."

A spark of interest appeared in Daisy's apathetic eyes. "Paw shore would wear 'em out, wouldn't he?" she ventured, not without relish.

Bertha looked at her. "Ain't you a fine sister, though? Standin' there wantin' your brothers to git into trouble!"

"I ain't," Daisy denied promptly, but her eyes fell.

"Don't you story to me, young lady. Shame on you! You tell them boys what I said or I'll see to it they ain't the only one that gits in Dutch."

"I'll tell 'em," Daisy said, alarmed.

"Git at it, then." Bertha turned back to her cooking, the old sickness swelling at her throat. "Seems like there ought to be somethin' I could do," she muttered as she banged the door of the warming-oven, where she had set the platter of ham and eggs to keep hot for the meal. "I can't git a-hold of 'em—none of 'em." A deep sigh stirred her, and she lifted her heavy knot of hair to wipe the streaming perspiration from her neck. "They ain't got nothin' to 'em *to* git a-hold of," she concluded despairingly.

She might well thank her lucky stars, she supposed, if she got the girls safely married without worse trouble than this constant sticky swirling and bubbling of jealousy and spite. She knew that most of her neighbors considered Opal a pretty girl, and a pretty girl was always in great danger.

Opal, mature for her twelve years, was already an accomplished coquette. She had a numerous train of gangling hickory-shirted swains, not to mention several grown men who followed her movements with more than casual interest. Fully aware of the profitable play to be made by wide, challenging blue eyes, moist, smiling lips and burgeoning, creamy-skinned body, Opal would have spent hours before the whorled mirror if Bertha had allowed her to; for, although entirely satisfied with herself in all other respects, she complained endlessly of her nondescript hair, which, frizzle and preen as she might, would make no effort to rise above its obvious destiny. "I'm a-goin' to have the darned old stuff dyed," she would threaten belligerently, yanking at a handful of it with vicious energy, "the very nex' time Paw says I can go to town."

"You jest let me ketch you," Bertha would retort. "A pretty-lookin' thing you'd be. You and Mamie Johnson. You want to be took for a bad woman?"

"I'd sooner be took fer a bad woman than a old stringy mop dressed up in clo'es!" Opal had burst out on the last such occasion, pulling her hair angrily. She glanced with some wariness at her mother, whose ire, she knew, could be safely roused only up to a point. "Mamie Johnson has a better time than I do, I bet," she muttered.

Bertha had made short work of shutting her up, but she did not speak again of Mamie Johnson. She was afraid to.

As always, Daisy had stood biting her nails in the background, listening with silent and concentrated interest. Daisy absorbed information as a sponge takes water. She never said anything about what she had learned until she could make it serve her purpose, but she remembered everything, and Opal, although she slapped her little sister out of her way casually enough when she had nothing in particular on her conscience, was not without a certain measure of respect for the younger child's deadly and malicious canniness. Daisy in her turn admired Opal's airs and graces and imitated them as far as she dared.

Bertha, hotly and constantly resentful of her bafflement, was still completely baffled. She had long ago fallen back on the only resource known to her, blind and unreasoning authority. She put up with the children's wrangling until she could bear it no longer and then arbitrarily stopped it, by force if necessary. She had never known a family in which there was no fighting, but for some reason unclear to her she could not take her own children's fighting for granted. Was it actually worse—had it really a more virulent quality— than the fighting in other families, or did her inordinate suffering over it spring from her hatred of Tim and the resemblance to him she saw in his offspring?

In the case of Clovis and Woodrow the latter might well be true, for they were replicas of Tim. In the other children the resemblance was more fleeting—a glance, a shrug, a sudden spitefully snarling tone. Only in Clarence was there no resemblance whatever.

And Clarence....

Clarence, she knew, had "something to him" to "git a-hold of" if he would only let her get near him. But he kept himself to himself. Again and again she had seized a quiet moment to try to win him, but always he withdrew in sullen distrust.

Why did he resist her when she loved him so? What had she ever done to him, that he should look at her with the eyes of a stranger? The old, endless aching pressed upon her. "If I only had some money that was mine," she thought wistfully, "I could git him a good fiddle. That there old thing he's got ain't no account."

But she knew there was no use in asking Tim for money for a fiddle. There was no use in asking Tim for anything. When Tim gave, it had to be his own idea, so that he could spread himself and strut. "He don't keer nothin' about givin' pleasure to nobody," Bertha told herself acridly, by no means for the first time. "He jest wants to feel like he's a-settin' on God's own cracker barrel fer a spell."

She heard him bawling an order now to Clarence as the two approached the house. What was it this time? Suddenly she knew. She had forgotten to unbridle Jess and put her in her stall. She braced herself doggedly for his half-jeering, half-furious recriminations.

Tim, however, had decided instead to ignore her, a form of punishment he resorted to occasionally. He came into the kitchen and drank noisily and at some length from the granite-ware dipper in the water bucket, then sat down in thunderous silence to wait for her to set his dinner before him.

Bertha watched him covertly, wondering, as she had wondered a thousand times before, how it was that she found herself married to him and bearing his children. "I reckon there ain't no reason," she concluded at length, drearily, "exceptin' I was jest a little fool too young to know what I was a-doin'. He certainly wasn't no pretty feller even then."

And certainly Tim was "no pretty feller" now. He was short and stooping and bull-necked, with a simian length of arm and a simian quality, too, in his heavy face. He was less unattractive sober than when he smiled, for his teeth were badly broken and marred with decay. Moreover, his smile was a cruel one, called into play for the most part only when he had someone at his mercy. When he assumed geniality for social purposes it was impossible to dissociate his smile from the one Bertha knew so well, the one that invariably doubled Clarence's hands into fists so hard that the knuckles stood out white. Had Bertha known it, her own hands followed suit on each occasion. "You stubborn, ornery bitch," Tim had grated at her the week before at the family table, and Bertha, too much alarmed at the boy's involuntary forward movement to feel any resentment for herself, had flung aside every thought but the need to pacify him before he noticed Clarence.

Now, as he sat there waiting for his dinner, knife and fork upright in his hairy fists, his face and neck red from the sun in the fields, his wiry grayish stubble of hair damp with sweat, she found it necessary again to be silent and appease him, for Clarence had slunk in at the back door and was waiting, alert, for his father's rage to break forth. Bertha served Tim quickly, called the other children in and, sitting down with Ardeth on her lap, began to feed her swiftly and efficiently, setting her down at last on the floor with a piece of transparent ham fat to chew on.

The meal proceeded in silence except for Tim's loud suckings and grindings. The children, quick to notice their father's mood, said nothing but ate steadily and unobtrusively, their eyes averted. Even Opal, who had been known to venture farther at such times than any of the others dared, was prudently silent. Clarence ate heartily but without interest, looking at nobody, his eyes bent glumly on his plate.

Bertha was nerving herself for an annual ordeal. She looked at her husband. "School starts a-Monday," she said at length, clearly and with meaning.

Tim paid no attention to her. The children looked up expectantly.

Bertha's face flushed with anger. "I said, school starts a-Monday," she repeated. "They can't go to school without no decent clothes, can they?"

Tim glared at her. "They can go to school stark nekkid fer all I keer," he snarled; but he reached into the pocket of his jeans and threw her a greenback. Bertha looked at it as it lay on the table. "It ain't enough," she said.

"By God it better be." Tim pushed back his chair, wiped his mouth on the back of his hand, and left the room.

The children's eyes, all but Clarence's, were fixed on their mother's face. Bertha's impulse was to scream, to swear, to fly at them in their helplessness and scourge them mercilessly with her own; but she said nothing and did nothing except to pick up the money and drop it into the pocket of her apron.

Tim's departure from the house, followed almost at once by Clarence's, set the younger children chattering in relief. One more crisis had passed them harmlessly, and they easily forgot it in the babble of jeers and recriminations that made up nearly the whole of their intercommunication.

Bertha's tension knew no such relief. Each time she steeled herself for combat and no combat arose, she knew a baffled fury that was half disappointment. "A body'd think I *liked* to have him blow off at me," she thought, nonplussed. "I don't know what's the matter with me, anyhow!" A furious shriek from Clovis penetrated to her consciousness. "Shet up!" she ordered the quarreling children, her eyes blazing. "Shet up and git out o'here, before I skin you alive! Yap, yap, yap, yammer, yammer, yammer! It's enough to drive a body crazy—"

She realized that the children were no longer there, that she spoke to an empty room. She drew a long breath, lifted and let fall her shoulders in exasperation, and set about clearing the table.

II

The Mallorys were newcomers to Weary Water. Tim had been a tenant farmer on several successive places in Arkansas, without profit or peace to anyone concerned. Owner after owner had evicted him, even in a region where shiftlessness in a tenant was more or less the expected thing. As a matter of fact, Tim as a farmer was less shiftless than many another, but his arrogance and bluster, or, as the whim took him, his sullen silent furies, wore upon the nerves of the most indulgent. At long last an uncle of his had died without an heir, leaving him the scrubby little farm in the Missouri swamp settlement, and he had moved his family there late in May, too late for the children to enter the Weary Water school during the current term.

Bertha accepted the change with stoic resignation. The Weary Water farm was no great shakes, but at least they could count upon keeping it. That the wretched little settlement was a sinkhole of infection, malaria, typhoid and dysentery, that poverty and illiteracy held undisputed sway, that there was not a book in the community except the Bible and the Sears-Roebuck catalogue, and that very few of the native inhabitants could read either of these were facts that deepened but little the dreary coloring of her existence. She read well enough herself, but the occasional bits of printed matter that had come her way were not of a sort to cause her to set much value upon them.

The Weary Water schoolmaster, Thomas Jefferson Plant, had been away all summer. She saw him now for the first time at Boney Bartlett's general store, where she was painfully gouging stockings for the twins and a gingham dress length for Daisy out of the meagre fund with which Tim had supplied her. She looked at him with gingerly intentness from the corners of her eyes as she bargained, for she had heard strange things about him. He was a "towner" and had a towner's notions, and the local worthies did not scruple to make sport of these to his face. "Give Mr. Plant his way," one of the men might observe, aiming a stream of tobacco juice expertly at a fly on the nearest wall," and your ol' woman'd have to bile every god-derned bucket o' water she drawed outen the river afore he'd let you take a drink. And screens! Hey, Mr. Plant, they ain't no screens on Wilkerson's backhouse yit. Hadn't you better git up there and fix 'em up right?"

Tim, in his more expansive moments, had recounted these incidents derisively at home, and Bertha, saying nothing, had taken the hint. She had religiously boiled all the family's drinking water ever since. She knew Tim too well to tell him what she was doing. When she screened the open windows with cheesecloth, there was a scene; but fortunately Tim was interrupted when he set about tearing the cloth away, and a night of sleep unbroken by mosquito bites had apparently made him think better of it.

Plant was buying sulphur ointment, a staple commodity and a pedagogic necessity in Weary Water, where a child whose fingers were not spread and oozing with "the itch" was a rarity. Misled by his thoughtful expression and his horn-rimmed spectacles, Bertha put his age at about thirty-five—an error. He was not yet twenty-seven. He was tall and spare, with a broad, high forehead, brown hair, and humorous mouth. His grey eyes, even through his glasses, were remarkably clear and penetrating. He was the only man in the place not in overalls and a hickory shirt, but he was not "dressed up," either; at least he did not look uncomfortable, and Bertha had never seen a dressed-up man look otherwise. Something about him suggested a gentleness she did not associate with masculinity, though his shoulders were broad and his hands looked very strong in spite of being as smooth and white as a woman's.

"That's all, Boney, thanks," he said to the storekeeper as he paid for the ointment and turned toward the door.

"He don't walk like no woman, anyhow," Bertha decided. "Nor he don't sound like one when he talks, neither."

The door swung to behind him. Bertha turned back to Mrs. Bartlett, who was cutting off the gingham for Daisy's frock. "That there's the teacher, I reckon."

"Yeah, that's him. Kind of a pretty feller, ain't he?" The woman glanced up suddenly and shrewdly at Bertha, whose face instantly became as passive as a sphinx's. "Hain't never ben married yit, neither."

"How do you know he ain't?" asked Bertha skeptically. "Maybe he's married a'ready and his woman backed out of comin' with him."

"He tole Boney he was a single man, time he applied. Boney's on the school board. Boney he says Mr. Plant wouldn't be here hisself, only fer the time he gits off to write. He's a-writin' a book, Boney says."

Bertha, smitten to the core with an astounding revelation, barely controlled a visible start. Never in her life, up to this lightning moment, had it occurred to her that books were written "by hand." She was numb with the shock of it, and with the additional shock of her own ignorance. "I'd jest like to know where I thought they come from," she ruminated, self-contemptuously. "I ain't never saw none growin' on a cornstalk yit." She interrupted Mrs. Bartlett's account of what she had said to Boney. "Is he a good teacher?" she demanded.

Mrs. Bartlett, a little resentful, shrugged her shoulders. "I reckon he's all right of a teacher. The young 'uns likes him."

"Where does he board at?"

"He don't board nowheres. Keeps bach for hisself down there in one o' Jed Baker's shacks down around the Bend."

Bertha digested this. The men she knew did not live without women to cook and clean for them. "Looks like he'd git lonesome thataway," she commented.

Mrs. Bartlett leered. "Maybe he does. Maybe you better go ast him."

There was a spiteful titter from the four or five other women in the store, but Bertha paid no attention; she was thinking of Clarence. "Does anybody ever go down there to see him?"

"Brother Pointer, he does oncet in a while, and sometimes ol' Doc Brumbaugh." Mrs. Bartlett's dull eyes narrowed. Dr. Brumbaugh, who did not live in Weary Water but was a frequent visitor, a sort of medical circuit rider, was the community atheist, and children and chickens fled at his approach. Even the stub-tailed setter that followed him was an object of terrified awe. "Some says we hadn't ort to keep a teacher that don't know no better'n to keep company with a infidel. But Boney, he says teachers is hard to git. Specially men teachers."

Bertha privately thought this very likely. In the first place, teaching was considered a woman's job, and the men of Weary Water, although they liked Mr. Plant, held him in good-natured contempt. In the second place, the post was meagerly paid and involved being on call at all hours of the day or night, for any conceivable emergency. There was no resident preacher, nurse or physician; everything devolved upon the teacher, from helping a farmer rescue a mired mule to playing the organ at revivals and laying out the dead. "Must be some feathers a-flyin' if Brother Pointer and Doc Brumbaugh gits there the same day," she suggested, more from a desire to prolong the conversation about Plant than from any interest in Dr. Brumbaugh and the pastor.

"I mean." The storekeeper's wife laughed shortly. "Sister Cory, though, she won't have nothin' to do with Mr. Plant as

long as he lets Doc Brumbaugh come to see him. Her last
revival she was a-preachin' at him somethin' awful."

"Sister Cory?"

"Sister Cory Plummer. She's our other preacher. She ain't
been here sence you come, I reckon; she don't git to Weary
Water as much as Brother Pointer does. She's a right powerful preacher, though. The Sperrit taken hold of her one day
when she was a-milkin' her old Jersey cow and tole her to git
out and preach the gospel and she's been a-doin' it ever
sence. She don't think much o' Brother Pointer's preachin'.
He don't make God out mean enough to suit her."

Bertha, whose interest in preachers and revivals was but
tepid, paid for her purchases and went home. That afternoon, as she slashed and stitched at Daisy's frock with the
nervous rapidity that characterized all her movements, her
thoughts returned and returned to Mr. Plant and his mysterious difference from the men she knew. "The young 'uns
likes him," Mrs. Bartlett had said. Would Clarence like him?
Could he tell her how to manage Clarence? Was it possible
that, in addition to his clairvoyant knowledge of the relation
between sickness and dirty drinking water, the teacher had
access to the deeper sources of knowledge she knew she
needed? "I wisht I could talk to him awhile," she thought as
she bit off her final basting thread and called Daisy in to try
on the dress.

But women did not talk to men in Weary Water except in
the presence of their husbands, and in Tim's presence she
could not talk of Clarence. "Some o' these days I'm jest goin'
to stop in there at Baker's shack and see him," Bertha told
herself.

This, however, she knew to be more than doubtful. It
would take more courage than she could be sure she had. In
the ordinary way of life she did not care what the other
women thought of her—of her fastidious housekeeping, her
children's aggressively clean, ironed clothing and unfester-
ing hands, her big ideas of herself as thereby denoted. But
even Bertha could not face without a qualm the rigidly
drawn moral distinctions of the community. If she went to

see Mr. Plant at his house, she knew, she might as well be Mamie Johnson and be done with it.

Maybe, if she rode Jess down around the Bend, she might meet him some day on his way to school. There was Opal as well as Clarence to worry about.

The notorious Mamie Johnson lived in Milltown, a dismal offshoot of the main community where stood a dead and deserted sawmill, hostel only to occasional night-prowling vermin. Here dwelt the poorest of the poor, families whose decaying shanties held no furniture but discarded packing-cases of splintery pine, who lived exclusively on corn pone and pinto beans, and whose rickety children wambled through eight or nine years of feeble life, died, and were dolefully buried in shrouds of curtain calico to the accompaniment of loud pious wailing in assent to the will of God. A Milltown funeral was a grisly thing; death was death's ultimate in Milltown, if only because there was so little difference between death and Milltown life.

Brother Pointer, who had never heard of sanitation but whose Christlike mercy and patience knew no distinction between the dirty and the clean, labored ceaselessly among the Milltown people, denying himself often to semistarvation in their behalf, preaching and preaching, with indefatigable hope, the beauties of chastity and holiness to minds that had and could have no conception of either. Sister Cory Plummer, a somewhat more egotistic apostle, swooped down upon Milltown at periodic intervals to blast it with the cleansing fire of condemnation and chill its composite spine with threats of everlasting hell fire and brimstone; but Milltown, almost immediately placid when she had gone, was none the holier for her exertions.

Dr. Brumbaugh had once been young and enthusiastic and persevering, but he had sunk long since into the face-saving cynicism of the unsuccessful. "Let 'em go to the devil their own way," he often advised the teacher, who seemed chronically troubled about them. "You can't do anything with 'em. I can't. God Himself couldn't. Leave 'em alone.

First they fiddle, then they pray, then they die—so call it a day!'' The old renegade would chuckle and clap the teacher on the shoulder. "As for poor old Mamie, she's about the only bright spot they've got to look at—her and her fancy furniture. *She's* got furniture." He chuckled again. "She's got lace curtains now. She's got 'em all tied up with pink ribbons." He lit his vile-smelling pipe and inhaled the resulting miasma with serene enjoyment. "I never worry about 'em any more, beyond giving 'em a pill or a tonic when they ask for it. No use."

"The Johnson woman's diseased, isn't she?" Plant suggested.

Brumbaugh shrugged. "Probably. So's half the rest of Milltown. What of it?"

These things, and many others like them, Bertha had heard. They were always in her mind nowadays when she thought of Clarence. The Milltown dances were savage orgies, full of drunkenness and violence, and she was not sure that Clarence did not even now slip out sometimes by night with his fiddle to play for them. It was altogether probable, for Tim would give the boy no spending money.

And there was little to choose, she thought, between the dances and some of the revivals. The Milltown element at revival time was hungriest of all, apparently, for salvation, but she had seen the boys and girls after the meetings, their eyes bright and their breath coming short with excitement, steal away to the sheltering woods together. Shotgun marriages and illegitimate births were the frequent outcome of such an emotional rending as religion provided here. It almost seemed as though Brother Pointer, a man of God if ever there was one, set loose upon the community the very evils against which he labored with such unceasing patience.

Bertha did not pretend to understand it. She had nothing against religion for those who liked it, and she believed without question what she had been taught about heaven and hell, taking it bluntly for granted that she herself, being insensible to the magnetic power of the Spirit, was "lost" unless some unexpected miracle should intervene. If it seemed strange to her that Tim, who shouted hallelujah with the loudest, should be assured of salvation in the midst of his mean and malevolent proclivities, it was no stranger than many another thing—no stranger, for example, than the fact that she, a mother concerned for her children, could seek no aid or comfort from the only source of aid and comfort she could perceive without being instantly classified as a fallen woman. These things were; that was all there was to it.

She knew that some of the people, when trouble assailed them, appealed to Brother Pointer for aid and comfort. "I'd jest like to know why," she informed herself hotly. "All he can do is tell 'em to pray to God—and a lot God cares what's the matter with 'em!"

She felt slightly guilty at this, not toward God but toward Brother Pointer. She had not been long enough in Weary Water to know him well, but she knew intuitively, as everybody did, that the old man's faith was unassailable and his Christian love a thing to marvel at. Heartsick as the knowledge of Tim's behavior would make him, his horror of her own rebellion against God and denial of His love, to say nothing of her hatred of Tim, would be far worse, and she knew it. Even if he had any help to offer, which Bertha doubted, he would be too violently shocked and distracted to provide it. "I wisht to the Lord he'd pack up his preachin' and tote it outen here for good," she thought not infrequently. "I reckon he means all right, but he gives me the willies."

In actual truth she was afraid of him, and afraid of herself as long as he was near her; afraid of betraying a vow she unconsciously made every day of her life: that she would yield respect to no man on God's earth. To one starved for kindness, as Bertha was both on her own behalf and on the children's, Brother Pointer was a formidable antagonist. With his four-year-old granddaughter Molly, without whom he was seldom seen abroad, he had made his duty call on the Mallory's on their arrival, at a time when Tim was not present, and Bertha, putting up with this as a matter of necessity, had loosed upon him several rather pointed suggestions that this visit would be all the pastoral attention she required. They struck his innocent mind and bounced back like children's darts from a plate-glass mirror, leaving no trace whatever. The only hint he took was one without words; he had seen her flinch when he called her Sister Mallory, and he had never once done it again.

"It's funny how he knowed that, when he never knowed a one of them other things I tole him," she thought, in momentary bafflement.

But she was already beginning to know him. "He jest don't listen," she concluded, "if you say anything mean to him. He don't b'lieve it, nary a word of it; he ain't got no notion on earth you done it a-purpose." Such trust in other people, who in Bertha's opinion could not be trusted any farther than you could swing a mule by the tail, was irritating; indeed it was more, it was downright appalling. If she didn't keep out of his way and keep him out of hers, she would wind up trusting him like everybody else, "like I didn't know B from a bull's foot," she thought angrily.

The bitter taste of frustration filled her, seeming to spread from her palate downward through her whole powerful body, as she twisted and turned Daisy about and about, measuring the hem of the gingham dress. "Stand still, can't you?" she snapped to the fidgeting child. "I can't git it right thisaway, no more'n if you was a wigglin' fishworm. There. Take it off now, and give it here."

But when Daisy had taken the dress off and gone, she dropped it in her lap and did not touch it. Her thoughts drifted back to the teacher. "I'm a-goin to go see him anyhow," she muttered to herself again. "There ain't nothin' else I c'n do."

Even this valiant decision, however, was long deferred in fulfilment—long, that is, for a woman of Bertha's habitual force and decision on all questions not related to Clarence or Tim. Nervous in spite of herself at the thought of "talk", even from women she held in utter contempt, and bewildered past coherent thought by the unaccountable differences she saw between Mr. Plant and all other men she had known, she was daunted anew by the words "He's a-writin' a book" and by her own ignorance as revealed by her astonishment.

"I ain't got no sense," she told herself repeatedly. "I knowed God written the Bible. 'F I'd 'a' had the brains He give a goose I'd 'a' knowed somebody must 'a' wrote the rest of 'em, even that'n."

"That'n" was the Sears-Roebuck catalogue, which lay on the undershelf of the center table in her "front room." She hauled it forth, sat down and spread it open on her knees, reading this or that description and turning the pages. "That ain't no kind of a job for a grown man to do," she thought disgustedly. "Looks like it'd drive a person crazy, if'n he wasn't crazy to start with."

Were the Weary Water men right, after all, in calling the teacher crazy, with "all them notions about winder screens and sech?"

There were "winder screens" in the catalogue, she knew; she turned up the pages and looked. "If he's writin' a book, I bet this here's where he gits 'em," she thought.

But no, that couldn't be it. Whoever wrote the descriptions in the catalogue must have had to "git 'em", the crazy notions, or facts, whichever they were, somewhere else in the first place, in order to write about them at all. "Gits 'em outen other books, like as not," Bertha ruminated.

What other books? What other books could the man find, and where would he find them? There was the Bible, everybody knew that, and there was the catalogue, and there were school books, of course: she had had those herself, and the children had them now. She had not so much as looked at one since leaving school to be married. "Seems like I can't remember what they was in 'em, neither: I wisht I could. I wisht to goodness Clance or Opal or somebody'd bring one home. I b'lieve I'll tell Opal to. The one they have to stand up and read out loud."

But she did not really believe it, and she was right. For some reason she could not even begin to explain even to herself, the idea embarrassed her. "Opal's so all-fired flip, she'd want to know why. And Daise would be standing there chewin' her nails and watchin'. It'd make me feel like a fool."

As for asking Clarence, he'd certainly think she'd gone crazy, or, if not that, that she was in cahoots with the teacher against him. "I don't b'lieve Mr. Plant's aginst Clance or anybody else," she argued with herself. "He don't look that way to me. But Clance, he thinks ever'body's aginst him, even me; and he won't gimme no chanst to prove it to him I ain't." She sighed deeply, replaced the catalogue on the shelf, glanced at the clock and went to the kitchen to begin preparations for supper, her heart aching as usual at thought of the boy's strange ways and her bitter memories threatening, also as usual, to blot all else from her mind.

This time, however, it could not. The approach she had made to thinking on abstract matters, to which heretofore she had been as little given as anyone else in Weary Water, had both startled and trapped her; she could not stop thinking now. "First thing you know I'll be gittin' them notions myself," she reflected. "Seems like if you let one in, all the rest of 'em's hell-bent to git in too, like a swarm o'gnats or mosquitoes or somethin'. I'll bet you my bottom dollar"— she paused, again startled, in peeling the potato she held— "that that there's what's the matter with Mr. Plant. He's let 'em all in, and now he can't git 'em out."

Her "bet" was instantly a conviction that nothing could change. She found this strange, but exciting. She stood there unmoving, the potato and the knife in her hands. "That's it, jest as sure as shootin'," she concluded. "That's why he don't seem like a man—not a real man, anyhow. Them notions has got him. He's let 'em git in and he can't make 'em git out."

She resumed peeling the potato, but her head fairly swam with novel conceptions. "Maybe he don't *want* to git 'em out," she thought suddenly, and stopped again. "Come right down to it, what's there *to* it, bein' a man? Look at Tim; he's a man, ain't he? Maybe Mr. Plant don't *want* to be a man. I shore wouldn't, I c'n tell you that. Or maybe in town they's differ'nt kinds o' men. It ain't likely, though."

She pondered. "Maybe—" her mind leaped clean out of bounds as a new thought struck her— "maybe he's *better'n* a man instid o' not bein' as good. You can't prove he ain't. Maybe he knows how to be a man and *then* some. Some o' them notions works, because I've tried 'em. My kidd don't git sick half as much as the other ones does, not sence I started boilin' that river water like he said." She started peeling the potato again, suddenly realized that the peeling was gone and that a long white strip of pure potato was lengthening beneath the knife, and laughed aloud. "Tim, he'd have a fit if he seen that," she chuckled as she plunged it into the water out of sight, "but what he don't know won't hurt him, and I don't keer two whoops. I wouldn't keer if'n I 'a' peeled it all away, no more'n a rabbit."

This superb indifference surprised her, but not for long. "Why, I been a-havin' a right good time," she thought and smiled. "I bet Mr. Plant does too; I bet he likes them notions. I shore would like to talk to him awhile. I'm a-goin' to, too, some o' these days, you see if I don't. I don't keer if he's writin' a catalogue twicet as big as that'n, I don't b'lieve he's got the big head about it. I bet it would be right nice to git to know him. Clance he likes him, no differ'nce what he makes out. I c'n tell."

The thought of the catalogue still turned her mind toward disgust, but she conquered it quickly. "That there ain't no job for a man. Mr. Plant'd know that. He wouldn't waste no time a-writin' that there. I wisht I knowed what kind of a book it is. I don't even know what kind of books people writes. Maybe he'd tell me, if'n I give him the chanst."

A deep-rooted longing, utterly strange to her, took possession of her mind and emotions. "Some kinds is bound to be worth it, or he wouldn't write 'em." Memory instantly confirmed her: "Boney says Mr. Plant wouldn't be here hisself only fer the time he gits off to write." Why, no, of course he wouldn't. Mr. Plant had come out from town, where in Bertha's untutored imagination everyone dwelt in luxury and ease, whatever trivial inconveniences they had to put up with. "Why would a towner come down here to live, unlest he had him a mighty good reason fer it? He ain't even got nobody to talk to, nobody but the school kids—and maybe old Doc Brumbaugh. They say Doc's smarter'n most people is around here. I reckon that's why Mr. Plant keeps comp'ny with him, infidel or no infidel. Ner I don't blame him, neither. I would too, if'n I had a chanst to." She glanced involuntarily upward, as was her unconscious habit when her thoughts skirted the sulphurous edge of blasphemy; but also, quite as usual, nothing happened. "I don't b'lieve God keers what people thinks and Doc shore don't. I wouldn't be surprised if they was two of a kind."

The picture of God and Doc Brumbaugh as two of a kind tickled Bertha immensely. It surprised her, too, for never before in her life had she been moved to laughter by anything her own mind conceived. It made her a little drunk, and in her mind she supplied God with a smelly pipe and a half-tailed dog, and pictured them cronies, swearing and laughing boisterously together.

Nevertheless, despite the release and intoxication of learning that her mind could be played with, "like one of Ardeth's play-pretties", Bertha found it no easier to take her reputation in her hands and visit the teacher. On the contrary, it was soon a great deal harder even to contemplate it. Her reasoning, though unpracticed, was quick when once aroused, and her musings on Mr. Plant's superiority to other men—Bertha set no Weary Water limitations; she was thoroughly convinced now that Mr. Plant was better than any other man, anywhere—had necessarily introduced a certain awe. More and more surely, as her speculations grew, she was convinced that his book, whatever it was, must be as much better than other books as he was better than other men, and therefore little, if anything, short of miraculous. Over and over and over again the wail of her ignorance maddened her. "I don't even know what differ'nt kinds o' books.... I wouldn't know *how* to talk to him! A person hadn't ought to *have* to feel like that there. It ain't fair. I'd like to know what God thinks He's up to, anyhow. If'n He loves people, like Brother Pointer says, He shore picks out a funny way to show it. Brother Pointer! He don't know. He don't know nothin'. He ain't got no more sense than I've got myself. Maybe not as much. Give him a lick o' sense and he'd know they ain't no God that *could* love people, not unlest He was a borned fool to begin with."

Nor was this nagging, torturing sense of inadequacy the only lion in the path. Bertha had enjoyed, and consciously enjoyed, her brief but enchanting parley with her mind, but she was not aware of any volition on her part; it had just happened to her, that was all. Maybe it would happen again and maybe it wouldn't. The chances were against it. "If'n Mr. Plant had 'a' been here when it happened, I could 'a' talked to him then, maybe," she reflected drearily in the days that followed.

She did not know why she thought so, and made no effort to find out. She had never concerned herself with the "why" of anything, with the sole exception of Clarence's distrust. She did not know that she had been, for a moment, set free—free of herself, to whom she did not know she was in bondage. That the barriers she attributed to Mr. Plant were in fact her own did not occur to her, and small wonder, for Tim was in a vile "humor" during this time, and all her strength and every resource she could lay hands on were needed to protect the children, as best she could, from violence, to say nothing of shielding Clarence from himself as well as from Tim. A new terror has assailed her after her last set-to with the boy, when she had noticed how fast Clance was growing, how nearly a man he was, how like a young stallion in strength and in fury as well, and what might come of the simmering hostility between the two men if manhood in Clarence should suddenly burst from the boy.

If'n I didn't have all them other young 'uns to look out for," she thought resentfully, "I c'd handle the two of 'em, maybe. But what can a person do? How do I know whicha-way Tim's fixin' to light? I can't stand it to see him light on the other young 'uns neither; I jest can't stand it. Nobody couldn't, unlest they was mean as Tim is." So ran her desolate thoughts in moments of respite; in moments of crisis red rage took her, body and soul, and after one of them a new devil confronted her, leering. "It might not be Tim that done it, ner Clance neither," she thought somberly. "It might be me. I wouldn't be surprised.... I wisht Brother Pointer'd shet up about that God o' his'n, oncet in a while, anyhow. He makes me sick at my stomach!"

What Bertha meant by "it" she preferred not even to think of; but she thought she knew the reason, now, why Brother Pointer and his long-suffering God made her "sick at her stomach." In a moment of the weakness she had feared, she had indeed "give in" and resorted to prayer, and had hardly got off her knees before Tim burst in and, seeing the twins in his path, knocked them both down and kicked them unconscious before she could reach them.

She hated Tim no more for his senseless sadism than she hated herself for that yielding. "If'n I hadn't 'a' done it, I could 'a' got there in time. It's a good thing that crazy old fool wasn't hangin' around nowheres near me; I'd 'a' knocked him flat as sure as you're born, and maybe killed him. I could, all right. I could kill him with one hand; he ain't got much stren'th."

A long, weary shudder went through her from head to foot. "It's a good thing he *wasn't* nowheres around just then," she thought. "Like as not he'd 'a' ketched me a-prayin', like a fool, and I'd never 'a' heerd the last of it, long as I live."

III

The swamp had known a brief period of loveliness in the spring, when trilliums and hepaticas covered the raw ground. It would be beautiful again in winter, with snow setting out the gnarled trees and crippled fences in patterns as wild, as mysterious with secret life, as a landscape painted in an opiate dream. But now, under the terrible down-bearing heat of late summer, it lay inert and panting in the sun, its hard rutted roads choked with yellow dust, its trees baked saffron and standing motionless. Straying hogs slept uneasily along its roadsides, their mud-caked sides heaving and twitching against the attacking flies. Windows and doors, most of them screenless, hung wide open to catch any faint breath of breeze that might be vouchsafed them. Flat-breasted women moved sluggishly about their household tasks or toiled up the slimy banks of the river carrying heavy wooden pails of silt-clouded water, their eyes as blank and incurious as the eyes of a beast of burden. It could not be believed that only a few weeks ago, under the frenetic exhortations of Brother Pointer's latest revival, they had danced and wept and embraced one another in the ecstasy of the awakened Spirit.

Men tilled their grudging fields with rusty implements, sweating and swearing like so many prisoners digging with their finger nails at a dungeon floor. Untended children, sapped by the heat of any desire to play, quarreled and fought and subsided and fought again around the blistering cabins, and the lean and sorrowful hounds, seeking whatever shade there was to find, lay waiting in brute patience for the crisp air of autumn and the short, sharp rapture of the chase.

Only Brother Pointer, walking with his little granddaughter Molly across the fields on some pastoral errand, was placid with a placidity more than animal. Bertha Mallory, pulling Jess to a halt a little too late to escape him, saw him help the child over a fence and step across it himself, smiling at the little girl's delight over a clump of blossoming fennel.

"Them's the Lord Jesus' flowers, honey," he told her. "The Lord Jesus must 'a' ben a-walkin' over these here fields last evenin' before us. Wherever His blessed feet has been, there blooms them pretty flowers."

"Lord Yedus 'tep on a mouse," observed Molly, diving into the mass of weeds and bringing forth the tiny carcass of the little field animal. "See? Poor mouse. Why'n't Lord Yedus look whichaway He goin'?"

Brother Pointer smiled at Bertha. "She's sech a little thing, she don't know no better," he said. "Howdy, Mis' Mallory. All well at your house this beautiful mornin'?"

"Howdy, Brother Pointer." Bertha's tone was barely civil. "Yes, we're all as well as can be, I reckon, in this awful heat."

" 'Tis warm," Brother Pointer admitted patiently, with an uneasy glance down at Molly. "It's hard on her, after bein' so sick this spring. There fer a spell I was afeard I was goin' to lose her. She ain't right peart even yit."

"She's lookin' better," Bertha said unwillingly. It was hard for her to praise this child, who was so unlike her own. Little Molly Pointer, underfed and ill cared for, but walking free and fearless in the light of her grandfather's all-embracing charity toward man and faith in his impossible God, was yet so endearing a child that only to look at the sunlight glinting on her yellow head made the unhappy woman's heart ache fiercely. Molly knew no dread of any human creature; she laughed and loved, inquired and explored, as naturally as Daisy and Clovis and Woodrow whined and whimpered. Dogs, cats and farm animals followed her as though she had been a tiny St. Francis, and she accepted their companionship with the impartial, merry-hearted faith that calls the whole universe brother. Bertha stared down at her from the back of the restless mare, at once loving and hating her.

"I did think, bein's it's Saturday," Brother Pointer was saying, "I might go by and look in on Mr. Plant. But I seen the doctor a-goin' in." His gentle face darkened, and he sighed. "It don't do no good fer me to talk to the doctor—no good neither to me ner to him. He's a right good doctor, I reckon. He saved my little Molly's life. But he's a carnal man."

Bertha said nothing. Her heart had given a sudden leap at Brother Pointer's first words; if the preacher was going to see Mr. Plant, surely she could go with him! And she could talk before him, or at least try to. A preacher was not like other men. And now here he was changing his mind—"skeered off by the doctor!" she thought impatiently, quite forgetful that she herself had already ridden twice past the schoolmaster's house without dismounting, "skeered off" by hindrances not even visible.

Her disappointment made her contemptuous. "I d'no as I'd pass up a chanst to save a dyin' soul, if I was a preacher," she remarked scathingly.

Brother Pointer took the rebuke without rancor. He only looked at her and slowly nodded, as though what she had said were but the echo of what his own conscience had been telling him. "I know how it looks, Mis' Mallory, I know how it looks. It looks like I ain't fitten fer the work my Lord's laid on me; that it does. But He knowed I wasn't when He called me." He pondered for a moment, undecided. "Maybe I ort to go and try agin. He's a good doctor. I can't never fergit what he done fer Molly."

Bertha felt her hands, in spite of the heat, grow cold on the bridle. "Brother Pointer," she said nervously.

The old man looked at her, waiting. She forced the words from her one by one, her own voice sounding strange to her ears. "Do you think it'd be all—all right, you know, if I was to go along with you? I ben a-thinkin' maybe I'd talk to the teacher about Clance—I ben a-thinkin'—"

"Why, shorely, shorely," Brother Pointer said, innocently surprised at her confusion. "Mr. Plant'll be right glad to see you, Mis' Mallory, I know he will. You come right along."

She dismounted and walked beside him, leading Jess. The relief of his acquiescence, the excitement of the doubtful venture, filled her with a strange weakness; she was glad even of the presence of Molly, who had laid the field mouse back in the weeds and now trotted ahead of them, singing.

"She likes to go to Mr. Plant's house; she plays with his cat," the old man said absently, and sighed. "It's right hard fer me to listen to the doctor a-scoffin' and a-blasphemin' the blessed Sperrit of God," he added apologetically, and fell silent.

Bertha did not answer him. The teacher's house, distinguished from the rest only by a blossoming blue morning-glory vine and a few valiantly striving clumps of purple phlox, was now in view. Molly, at the sight of a large singed black and white cat on the stone doorstep, had broken into a run, her arms spread wide. "Chadderack!" she shouted.

"That there's the teacher's cat she sees," explained Brother Pointer. "Shadrach, they call him. Somebody treated him plumb mean before Mr. Plant found him; must 'a' throwed live coals on him, I reckon."

Bertha heard him but still did not reply. She could not. She knew, with half her consciousness, that Brother Pointer was talking against time and at random, fighting off his dread of his encounter with the doctor, but she had no attention to spare him now. She was trying desperately to shape the words in which she would speak of Clarence.

The teacher saw them coming and opened the screen door hospitably wide. "Hello, Molly. Yes, bring Shadrach in if you want to. Morning, Brother Pointer; how are you? Morning Mrs.—" he hesitated.

"This here's Mis' Mallory," Brother Pointer introduced her. "She—"

"Oh, yes, I know. You're Clarence's mother. Come in; I'm glad to see you." He looked at her keenly and kindly, and Bertha felt her mouth go dry with wondering joy. This was a marvelous man, a witch or something, she thought; he divined at once what had brought her here. He knew she had other children, but he said "You're Clarence's mother."

"Clance acts right ornery sometimes," she said faintly.

"It's the spring o' the year fer him, that's all," Brother Pointer put in with a palliating smile. "All young things is skittish. They don't mean no harm.... Mornin', doctor," he added courteously to a dense cloud of blue smoke rising from a chair in a corner of the room beside which sat a ragged shepherd dog with half a tail.

Brumbaugh grunted not unamiably in reply and hitched himself forward to bow to Mrs. Mallory. They sat down, Molly on the floor with the cat in her arms, her thin little shoulder rubbing affectionately against the old dog's flank. Brumbaugh regarded her critically through smoke. "Have an orange, Molly?" He pulled one from the pocket of his dingy seersucker coat. "Well, you look better. She looks better, Pointer." He nodded.

"Yes, she's better, bless the Lord." Brother Pointer's eyes were harried, for he knew what was coming, and he fumbled noticeably in search of a different and a safer topic. But the doctor was too quick for him.

"Ee-yup. She ought to do all right now if you don't feed her any more sausage and rotten bananas after she ain't had anything fit to eat for a week."

Mr. Plant, apparently experienced in these passages at arms, moved to the rescue. "Where've you been so early in the morning, Brother Pointer, on a broiling day like this?"

The old man turned to him in grateful relief. "I ben over to Milltown, Mr. Plant, to see that pore Williamson girl. I buried her baby a-Tuesday, you know." He shook his head. "She's a-takin' it mighty hard."

Brumbaugh grunted again. "Woods colt, wasn't it?"

"I'm afeard so; I'm afeard so." Brother Pointer emitted a long and deeply troubled sigh. "She's pretty much broke up—out of her head by times." He turned back to Plant, his voice suddenly rising in a passion of grief. "I am a wicked and slothful servant, Mr. Plant! I ain't done my duty even yit in that there house. It jest seems like I can't make myself do it. I knowed very well I ought to 'a' told that girl the Lord taken her baby away to punish her fer her sin. I ought to 'a' told her she was a sinner under condemnation; I ought to 'a' warned her to repent while there's yit time. But pore girl, pore girl! I jest couldn't. It seemed like I couldn't say a word—"

"Christ Almighty!" exploded the doctor, banging his pipe furiously on the arm of his chair. "Will you listen to this ding-blasted fool sitting here apologizing for every decent instinct he's got? I swear to God I don't know what religion's good for if it can't make God out nothing but a God-damned baby killer! I'd as soon worship old Shep here!"

Brother Pointer got slowly to his feet. "Don't you talk that way to me, doctor," he said in a tone of iron. "Don't you talk that way. You better look to yourself. You're a carnal man; your steps takes hold on hell. The anger of the Lord is slow a-comin', but you'll feel it when it comes. His wrath is a consumin' fire; it's death to the blasphemer, and He will destroy the tongue that takes His name in vain! He is more terrible than a army with banners! You mark my words the time'll come when you'll wisht you'd 'a' listened to me. I ben a-warnin' you, off and on, fer—"

Brumbaugh grinned. "I make it six years come Thanksgiving," he interrupted mildly. "Set down, Pointer. Set down and cool off." He turned to his host. "My apologies, Jeff. A preacher has to work at his trade, I reckon. I oughtn't to 'a' touched him off." He lit his pipe and looked across at Bertha. "You sing, Mis' Mallory?"

"Sing?" Bertha, startled, turned toward him. "Why, I—well, I used to, now and agin."

He nodded. "Thought you did. You look like a singer."

He rose and took down a battered banjo that hung on the wall. "Give us a tune, why don't you? They say music hath charms to soothe the savage breast. What d'you think will meet your needs at the moment, Pointer?"

But Brother Pointer, though he had sunk back in his chair, was deeply affronted and would say nothing. Bertha, helplessly accepting the banjo the doctor thrust upon her, looked uncertainly from one to the other.

"Do sing us something, Mrs. Mallory," Plant urged her. "Give us a ballad or"—he glanced at Brother Pointer—"a hymn or two. Do you know 'When the Saints Go Marching In?' "

"I used to," Bertha said shyly. She struck a chord and sang the first words falteringly; then, suddenly achieving self-forgetfulness, she let her voice come deep and full from her heaving bosom.

The three men stared, amazed at the passion in her voice. Jeff Plant's sensitive countenance wavered from surprise to excitement, then to a look of inner certainty, as though that glorious outpouring had confirmed some secret opinion. Brother Pointer forgot his grievance and sat up straight in his chair, his mystic's eyes alight. "Glory to God!" he breathed as she finished the first stanza. "Mis' Mallory, the blessed angels theirselves couldn't sing it no grander."

Dr. Brumbaugh glared at him. "Well, let her get on with it, can't you?" He looked at Bertha. "You've got a damned good voice," he said. "Go on—go on!"

But Bertha, fighting off the threat of tears, had got to her feet. Her mind was a whirlpool of incomprehensible, unfamiliar images and emotions; she had forgotten Clarence, and she had no idea why she was about to cry. She knew only that she must get away at once. "It's time to git dinner on the table," she faltered; and then, feeling the words to have been clumsy and perhaps offensive, she added with an effort, "You shore got a lot o' books here, Mr. Plant, ain't you?"

"You're welcome to read any of them, Mrs. Mallory, any time. Here, let me give you one, at least, to take with you." He glanced briefly over his five modest shelves, selected a book and handed it to her. "I think you'll like this. Keep it as long as you like, there's no hurry. And do come to see me again, either here or at the schoolhouse. I've been wanting to talk to you about Clarence."

Clarence? Clarence? Who was Clarence? Bertha swallowed desperately against a rising sob. She tried to return the teacher's clear, friendly gaze but could not; her eyes, stretched wide against the encroaching tears, went past him, over his shoulder to the top of the bookcase, where she saw for the first time a large framed photograph of a young and dark-haired woman, sitting at a desk or a table, her slender hands clasped upon it. "I—I got to go," she mumbled indistinctly, and fled through the open door to where Jess stood waiting.

She knew Mr. Plant was watching from the door, and as she tried to mount she stumbled and turned her ankle, wrenching it painfully. But at his exclamation and the sound of his approach she leaped desperately to the mare's back, ignoring the pain, and was gone. She heard him shout after her, "Mrs. Mallory! Are you all right?" but she did not look back.

IV

She rode blindly home, letting Jess choose her own gait. The fit of crying she had dreaded did not come on her after all. Her eyes were dry as she rode into the stable yard to unbridle the mare. The book in her hand surprised her, for she had not been aware of carrying it. She looked unseeingly at its title, *Nicholas Nickleby*. It meant nothing to her. She had not wanted it. She had spoken of the books only because she felt compelled to say something, and there they were, rows of them, more books than she had ever seen before, more books than she had ever known anyone had.

She could see them now in their slanting rows, their bindings broken and worn with use. The rest of the teacher's house was a blur in her mind. She could not have said what chairs there were, what tables or what pictures, except one. The woman's photograph was plainer to her now than it had been in full sight; she remembered it with a mixture of contempt and anguished envy—contempt for its slightness, its unnatural delicacy, and envy that burned like a branding iron for the same. It made her feel gross and solid, mountainous, and at the same time filled her with the certainty that she could put an end to the woman with one stroke of her hand, that she could mash the woman like a fly. "I'd like to, too," she found herself thinking savagely.

She shook herself all over impatiently, like a dog, and panted. What in tunket had got into her all of a sudden? She had never been so shaken before. She had never felt either this way or that way about herself; she had not had time. The tempestuous floods of emotion that constantly rocked her— hatred for Tim, adoration of the difficult Clarence, pity for her neglected other children, and scorn of her mouthing neighbors, poured out from her, never toward her; even her occasional self-contempt was somehow objective, the contempt of the spectator and the uninvolved. It was as though a total stranger had walked into her body. She did not know the woman, had never known her.

She had failed of her errand, had wasted, perhaps forever, her hard-won chance to talk with the teacher about Clarence. She thought of it now, but apathetically. "It don't make no difference. He knowed what it was I was after. He knowed it better'n I did myself, I reckon."

She was briefly amazed; how could this be? How could it? Well, but the teacher was not like other men. "I seen that myself, right away," she reminded herself. "I seen he was smart." But it was not his "smartness" that tormented her. It was his difference, and the rhyming, repetitive difference of the woman in the photograph. Two of a kind, she tried to think, and failed. The woman would look down on her, no doubt; "but I don't reckon Mr. Plant would." she thought miserably.

She picked up the book from the edge of a manger, where she had laid it while she put Jess in her stall, and carried it into the house, hiding it in the kitchen cupboard to avoid Tim's suspicious nagging. It disappeared from her thoughts as though it had never been. It was the smallest, most unnoticeable part of her memory of the visit. What absorbed and bewildered her was the torrent of new and disturbing emotion that rolled and tumbled about in her body and brain. She remembered that Clarence one day, when he was "good and mad", had struck a string of his fiddle so hard that its humming vibration could still be heard after he had put the instrument down and slammed out of the house. The sound, persistent, discordant and somehow frightening, came back to her, filling her ears. "I feel like I was that there string!" she thought, amazed.

She could not shake off her unease or recall herself to her usual vigorous routine. Although she answered the children when they called to her and attended as usual to her ceaselessly recurrent household chores, she did not fully hear anything that was said to her or feel her household implements in her hands. In the late afternoon the aching pulsation subsided, but nothing took its place. She sat down to rest for a few minutes before preparing supper. She heard Ardeth screaming like a siren and knew, vaguely, that Clovis was teasing her, but she said no word in protest.

That night, with Tim snoring noisily beside her, she remembered the book, and a dull curiosity took her. She could not sleep anyway, feeling like this. She slipped out of bed, flung on an old cotton wrapper over her nightgown, and groped her way to the kitchen. Lighting a lamp, she took the book from the cupboard and sat down noiselessly at the kitchen table. In five minutes she was absorbed.

It was the first novel she had ever read. The intolerable Squeers filled her at once with familiar loathing. "He's kind o' like Tim," she thought vaguely.

Yet it eased her, somehow, to read of him. "I reckon misery loves company, as they say. But it seems like somehow there's more to it than that."

She read on and on. At two o'clock, oppressed by the jostling multitude of new impressions, she put the book aside and slipped out into the yard, indefinably excited and as far from sleep as ever. Night had brought little abatement of the heat, but the moon, now full and round and luminous in the sky, threw an illusion of false coolness over the swamp. The tangled, dusty woods, coated with that impersonal silver, looked natural again, as they had looked in the forgotten springtime.

A man came whistling down the road from the direction of Milltown. She knew him. It was Bud Wilkerson. "At this time o' night!" she said to herself. "I bet he's been to see Mamie Johnson; I wouldn't put it apast him. Or some o' them Milltown girls."

Wilkerson was the established Lothario of Weary Water, a stalwart, not unhandsome man in his middle thirties, whose amorous exploits were second, in local interest, only to the revivals. His wife Lucy was a thin, broken-toothed slattern who looked old enough to be his mother, though she was actually several years younger than he and had married him, as was the custom of the region, while she was still no more than a child. The Wilkersons had several children, and Lucy matched her husband's prowess in other fields by her own histrionic superiority among the women when it came to childbearing. "My ol' woman shore can raise a hell of a racket when she's a-birthin'," Bud frequently boasted, as one who gives even the devil his due.

But he had no interest in Lucy beyond this periodic admiration. He seemed to take quite for granted the imperceptible changes that had altered her in a few short years from the pretty, bouncing hoyden she had been to the yellow-skinned, lop-haired, whinnying caricature of a woman she had become.

In this, Bertha knew, he was not unique or even peculiar. All the Weary Water men took these things for granted. Their own work in the fields, though arduous in season, left them the long winters to relax in, and they were not deprived by convention or drudgery of the additional ease to be found in the society of their neighbors at any time of the year. They hunted and fished; they whittled and made merry about the jovial base-burner at Boney Bartlett's store; they played poker or checkers with friends in their shanties in the evening, unoffended by the acrid-smelling, half-cleansed diapers drying on chairs and sawhorses behind the stove. They all looked years younger than the women they had married, but most of them, however they may have envied Bud his insouciant disregard of the community's disapproval and

Brother Pointer's diatribes, were at least physically faithful to their marriage vows.

With Bud it was different. He cocked an expert and estimating eye at every female creature beyond the age of eleven who crossed his swaggering pathway. Most of them, it is true, who were much past that age were supremely unappetizing; Bertha Mallory was the only mature woman of them all who held up her head—and had teeth in it—and whose body was outspokenly the body of a woman, rich with life. Bertha had marked his eyes upon her many times. For that matter, she had seen him eying young Opal again and again with eager and covetous interest.

She stood still now as he approached, thinking it less likely he would see her standing so than if she moved in the direction of the house. But Bud, even at two in the morning and after a presumably rewarding visit to Milltown, was not missing anything. He saw her.

"Evenin', Mis' Mallory," he said, coming to rest at the fence and leaning casually on his sinewy forearms. "Right hot yit, ain't it?"

"Evenin', Mr. Wilkerson," Bertha responded distantly and briefly.

"Now that there ain't hardly friendly." Bud took off his battered straw hat and passed a hand through his thick dark hair. "Ain't nobody hereabouts calls me Mr. Wilkerson. My name's Bud."

Bertha did not reply.

"That ol' moon up there looks kind o' lonesome, don't it? Pretty, though."

"Yes."

"Makes your hair look mighty pretty too, a-shinin' on it." He grinned ingratiatingly. "I was a-sayin' to Lucy here jest a while back, I says, I says, that there Mis' Mallory's shore got the prettiest hair of any woman ever come to these here parts."

Bertha made no answer.

"Shore is a pretty night," the man continued. "Seems like it calls fer a little somethin' extry, don't it?"

"Sech as a trip to Milltown?" Bertha suggested blandly.

Wilkerson was delighted; he chortled and choked with laughter. "Say, ain't you the quick one! Now, Mis' Mallory, what on airth ever made you think I'd ben to Milltown?"

"You was shore a-comin' from that direction when I first seen you," Bertha retorted, but without noticeable disapproval. She knew she ought to go in, but she found herself oddly excited and stimulated. She liked Bud Wilkerson in spite of herself. She could see what women found attractive in him. His gaiety and light-heartedness, in this environment, were alone enough to generate desire.

His open admiration, as he stood there gazing at her, was like a sudden bubbling of wine in her blood and senses. Unconsciously she posed for him, head up and bosom high. But as he moved to saunter toward the gate she was assailed by panic; Tim was a heavy sleeper but not an oblivious one. Besides, she herself didn't want—she didn't want—

She turned, with a hasty good-night, and hurried toward the house, leaving him standing open-mouthed but by no means discouraged still outside the fence. A moment later, peering warily from the kitchen window after she had put away her book and extinguished the light, she saw him strutting unabashed toward home, matching his prancing step to his high-hearted whistle.

She stared after him for a moment. "It'd serve Tim right if I did," she muttered as an explosive snore from her husband cut across her reverie. "Oh, well. The men's all alike, I reckon."

But she knew that it was not true. Bud Wilkerson was not in the least like Tim. With all his philandering, he was known to be kind and indulgent with Lucy and the children. He would be a blithe and adventurous, if inconstant, lover. There was no real harm in him. And Brother Pointer and Dr. Brumbaugh were different too, in their different ways, and so was Jefferson Plant.

She moved quickly away from her thought of the schoolmaster, for it made her obscurely ashamed of the little interlude with Bud. Here she was, an old married woman, a woman with six children, dickering in the dark with Weary

Water's champion rapscallion, and both of them fully aware
of what their banter implied. She was no better than any of
the rest of his fancy women. She was worse. She was Opal's
mother, and she knew that he had his eyes on the young
growing girl. Yet she had encouraged him; next time she met
him he would make his advances with even greater assur-
ance. "Spreadin' hisself like a banty rooster," she thought,
her cheeks hot.

She did not ask herself why the thought of Jefferson Plant
made her ashamed when the thought of Tim, her own husband, left her only revengeful. Bertha was not much given to
analysis, and even if she had been she would have been
hampered at every turn by her lack of words to clothe her
mixed emotions.

It was what held her back with Clarence. Loving him,
willing either to kill or to be killed for his sake, she could
find no speech that would penetrate his thick defenses. She
could only remonstrate with him in what language she
knew, and then, when his resentment rose, command or
threaten him, driving him farther and farther from her with
every word she uttered.

She settled back into bed beside the snoring Tim. "I
wisht—" she thought, and halted, for she did not know what
it was she wished. It was all a question, a dense and maddening blankness.

She remembered the book she had been reading before her
encounter with Wilkerson. There too, it seemed, in that
strangely captured world, were confusion and bewilderment, weakness and valor, foolishness and misery and anger
and pity and frustration. But how it marched, how it
marched upon the mind! "He shore knowed a-plenty,
whoever written that there," she thought, marveling again
that this miracle could be accomplished by a merely human
creature. It was like witch-work, a thing past comprehension.

Now that she had rested from the book's initial onslaught,
now that her later excitement had subsided and cooled, she
wished that she might finish it. But she must rest; there
would be work to do in the morning. Later, when she was all

through for the day, she would get back to it and read some more.

    She pushed her pillow into place and slept.

V

During the days and weeks that followed, the heat pressed down with such intense concentration as to fling aside all other discomforts, all other animosities, almost all other physical consciousness. No rain would fall. The air they breathed was powdery with dust. One of the Baker boys was overcome by sunstroke in his father's fields and hung precariously between life and death for three days. The other men, awed and swearing, knocked off work and got out their dilapidated fishing tackle. "Ain't no man can stand to work in this here," said Baker, wiping the sweat and grime from his face with a red bandanna; and the other men, who were accustomed to look to him, the largest landowner for miles around, as final arbiter in any dispute, agreed explosively and wiped their own sunburned necks in loud relief.

The women, of course, drudged on. Their men must be fed, their children tended; the catfish brought home must be cleaned for cooking. The hair of the women stuck to their wet faces, clinging spitefully to their equally wet fingers when they tried to push it away. Nobody could sleep, and the fretful cries of children tormented by the swarms of mosquitoes that came in through the screenless doors and windows made night a literal hell. The flat stones set in front of the houses for doorsteps, having baked all day long in the pitiless sun, were still hot to the touch at three o'clock in the morning. "Jesus!" the men muttered, not without certain stunned admiration, as they sat down upon these and got quickly up again.

In the Mallory shanty, Bertha, like the others, toiled stoically on. Tim had gone fishing with the rest, and the nauseating smell of catfish offal had constantly to be disposed of. The other women did not bother about it; they flung the entrails out upon the ground at a moderate distance from their shacks and left them to be set upon by flies. Bertha, digging pits to bury hers, treading the earth down upon it with all her strength, was an object of derision. "She shore must like to wear herself out," the women said.

But Bertha, hot, miserable and seething as she was, was in no real danger of wearing herself out. Exhaustion was a word she did not know. Her strong fine body served her will like steel, and her restless mind, pricked of late to new and strange activity, moved on its way like a separate thing, unaware of the bubbling caldron of heat within her.

The appetite aroused by *Nicholas Nickleby* was soon a demanding hunger that even prudence could not overcome. She carried the book back at last, one Saturday morning, to the schoolmaster's house. She would not enter, but she seized avidly upon the two other books he brought out to her, exclaiming with astonishment when she learned that the same man had written them.

"Oh, yes," Plant assured her, seeing her bewilderment. "He wrote a great many books. I thought, since you liked Nickleby, you might like the others as well as anything I've got."

"Is all of 'em different?" persisted Bertha, still surprised. "With different people in 'em?"

He smiled. "Oh, yes. That's the difference between a writer and a great writer, Bertha. Genius never dries up, like a pond; it goes on and on, like a river."

He did not notice that he had used her given name, but she did, and a pleased flush came into her cheeks. She had meant to ask what "genius" was, but forgot it. "Is the book you're a-writin' like these here?" she ventured, hesitantly. "I mean—Mis' Bartlett said you was writin' a book."

Jeff laughed. "I'm hardly in Dickens' class, I'm afraid. Besides, I'm not even a published novelist yet."

"A novelist?"

"Dickens—the man who wrote those books—was a novelist. All those books are novels. Long stories, you know, about life and people."

"Don't Brother Pointer say novels is wicked?" asked Bertha.

"Probably. But don't worry about these, Bertha. Brother Pointer hasn't read them. They're not going to hurt your immortal soul to any extent." He smiled again. "That same Holy Spirit Brother Pointer's so fond of talking about probably dictated most of them, word for word."

Bertha did not follow him. "I ain't got no immortal soul to hurt, I don't think," she said morosely.

He laughed. "Haven't you? What makes you think you haven't?"

"Well, I ain't never been converted." She looked questioningly at him. "I was to a lot o' meetin's—Tim takes on if I don't go whenever they have one. But the Sperrit ain't never took hold o' me yit. I don't reckon it's ever a-goin' to."

"I wish you'd come in and sing me a song," Plant said with apparent irrelevance.

Bertha took alarm at once. "I must git on home. The children's by theirselves." She turned away.

"Wait a minute." He touched her arm detainingly. "What are we going to do about Clarence, Bertha, when he gets through school here? He ought to go on to high school. And he ought to do something about his music. He's got too much talent to neglect. You don't want him going to seed here, wasting it all in playing for the dances at Milltown. He might do almost anything if he could get away."

Bertha twitched restlessly. "I reckon Clance jest thinks he can play," she objected. "And he's so all-fired ornery I can't do nothin' with him anyway."

"No. His talent is real and important. He's 'ornery', as you call it, because he needs to play. His own music, not Milltown's. Something must be done about it, Bertha."

"What kin I do?" she asked sullenly.

"Talk to him about it. Encourage him. And—" he hesitated—"if you could manage to get him a good violin—"

She was silent.

I'm no great judge of music," Plant went on. "But Dr. Brumbaugh's a better one—he used to want to play, himself—and he agrees with me that the boy has a chanc; the whole world might come to listen to him. You talk to Clarence about it. It'll help him just to know you're on his side." He paused, waiting, but she did not answer. "Well, that's all I wanted to say, Bertha. You think about it."

Bertha thought about it all the way home. She was walking, for one of Tim's mules had gone lame and he was using Jess in the fields.

Her thoughts had not much coherence or much purpose. In the first place, her impression of what the teacher thought Clance might do with his music was far too vague for definition. In the second, there loomed before her, as always, the stubborn breastwork of her husband's certain opposition. "I'd' no what makes him think," she fumed, meaning Plant, "that all a person's got to do is say 'One, two, buckle my shoe,' and everything'll be fixed."

But his words darted about in her mind and stung her, and late that afternoon, catching Clarence alone with his fiddle in the front room of the shanty, she drew a long breath and attempted to "encourage" him. "I mustn't git mad at him, now," she breathed, almost aloud, as she entered the room.

Clarence did not look up as she approached him. He finished the phrase he was playing, an odd one, it seemed to her, without much melody in it, and lifted the bow again as she stood there hesitant.

Desperately she interrupted him. "That sounded right pretty, Clance."

Clarence's heavy brows lifted for a moment, then fell. The bow in his hand trembled slightly as he brought it down.

"Clance." Bertha rubbed her wet palms down the sides of her apron.

This time he grunted a reply. "Yeah? What?"

"Clance, you don't never—you don't never—" Why was it so hard to talk to him? Why did his mere presence always bring this stammering fear? Her very love for him oppressed her with its weight, so that the words sank back as fast as she tried to speak them. But she got it out at last. "You don't never play fer them Milltown dances, do you?"

Clarence was startled; the bow wavered again. His eyelids flickered and he shot her a wary glance, as though considering whether it would be worth his while to lie. A tense moment moved past them. Finally, choosing counterattack rather than evasion, he said loudly, "Sure I do. All the time. What of it?"

Bertha advanced, venturing to lay her hand on his arm. "Don't you, Clance. I wisht you wouldn't." She struggled visibly for expression. "Them's not—them's not nice dances over there."

He dropped his eyes again. "Aw, what differ'nce does it make?"

Bertha drew a long breath. She had not got far, but it was better than it had ever been before. He was not shouting. He had not jumped up from his chair to hang his fiddle away and stamp out of the house.

"I was a-thinkin', Clance—" she began, and stopped again. "You'd like it if I could git you a good fiddle instid o' that there old one, wouldn't you?"

"You couldn't git me no good fiddle," Clarence stated coldly. "Good fiddles cost money. You got 'ny money?"

"I ain't got none now, but if I could git some—"

"Where you goin' to git it at? From Paw?" Clarence

laughed loudly and raucously. "Fat chanst!" He laid the old fiddle on his overalled knee and looked at her. "You been a-talkin' to Mr. Plant?"

She nodded. "Mr. Plant thinks—"

He mocked her, bitterly. " 'Mr. Plant thinks'. I know what Mr. Plant thinks. He ain't got no sense." The boy turned his head aside, staring woodenly out through the window. "I reckon he means all right, though."

"Clance, he—" Bertha moistened her dry lips. "He talked like he thought you might git to play the fiddle in a—a kind of show, I guess it is, up on a pulpit, like, and the people comin' to listen."

"Yeah." Clarence looked at her and then away, and added, as though the words were being wrung from him, "A concert, he calls it."

"Would you like it, Clance? That there—concert, is it?"

The boy's features worked. "Y' damn right I'd like it," he blurted, and, getting up, deliberately turned his back on her, his shoulders heaving; but he made no move to leave the room.

She came timidly near him and put her arm around him. He twisted himself fiercely free. "Lemme alone. Lemme alone, I tell you. It ain't no use. I wisht I was dead! I wisht I'd 'a' never ben borned! I wisht I'd 'a' never heerd o' Mr. Plant, or you neither!" He turned upon her, glaring. "If the both of you don't lemme alone, I'll—"

He lifted the fiddle as if to bring it down with all his force on the chair at his side, but she caught his arm in midair. "It's all the fiddle you've got, Clance," she said quietly, "don't break it." She took it gently from him and hung it on the wall.

He let her have it, his hand dropping limply at his side. His fury abated as suddenly as it had flared, and he stammered wretchedly, gropingly, "Maw—"

The tortured monosyllable was all Bertha's hungering heart had needed. She caught him close to her in a passion of love and rapture, and for a moment he submitted. When he broke away his face had hardened again, and her heart sank;

but at the door he turned, his mouth twisted awry, his hot eyes blinking back tears.

"I only played twicet at Milltown," he said in a muffled croak, and fled.

No lover's madrigal was ever sweeter to loved one's ears than these suffering syllables to Bertha. She knew what they meant, and the reluctant love that had prompted them sang in her soul. Ecstasy swayed her almost to falling where she stood; for a moment it seemed to her that the whole world had burst into song.

She herself sang, presently, when the first tide of joy had receded and she was herself again. Ardeth staggered into the room and caught at her skirts. She snatched the child into her arms and rocked her, sitting down with her in the rickety rocking chair, feeling again and again the hard, rebellious youngness of her son, the furious power within him, their essential unity. Her magnificent voice swept through the house like a gleaming, pulsating tide.

> *Rockaby, baby, in the tree top!*
> *When the wind blows, the cradle will rock;*
> *When the bough breaks—*

The astounded Ardeth, wishing to sit up and contemplate this unheard-of phenomenon but quite unable to wrest herself free of the strong arms that held her, and the other children, crowding cautiously to the door to watch, were smitten dumb. Bertha paid them no heed. She sang and sang, going from lullabies to ballads to revival hymns in a sort of mounting frenzy. Brother Pointer, passing the farm on his way home from the rounds of the day, was surprised but deeply gratified to hear the still unconverted Mrs. Mallory proclaiming exultantly in song,

> *I'm a-goin' to set down beside my Jesus,*
> *I'm a-goin' to set down and rest a little while.*

VI

Impulsively, on the ebbing but still glorious tide of this elation, she "tackled" Tim that evening after supper. "Tim," she began, her breast heaving, her eyes alight, "I was a-talkin' to the teacher here the other day—"

"Where at?" he interrupted her, his little eyes instantly suspicious. "He been here while I was out in the fields?"

Bertha bristled. "No, he ain't. I wisht you'd listen to a person oncet in a while! I was a-talkin' to him, and he says—"

Tim brought his fist down on the table. The children jumped. "I ast you, where at?" he bellowed at her. "If he ain't been sniffin' around here—" Opal snickered, but he silenced her with a look—"you ain't had no chanst to talk to him without you been trollopin' after him somewheres else! Whereabouts did you see him to talk to?"

Bertha trembled, but controlled herself. Across the table Clarence waited, tense. The appeal he would not make to her glared from his eyes: shut up, Maw, fer Godsakes let 'im alone! Shut up, shut up, shut up! But Bertha could not. She swallowed and plunged on. "I was a-ridin' right by his house, that's where I seen him. I ain't a-talkin' about the teacher, I'm a-talkin' about Clance—"

"I bet my bottom dollar you're a-talkin' about Clance," grated Tim, with a malignant glare in Clarence's direction. "I ain't ever seen you yit when you wasn't. All right, since you're so set on talkin' about Clance, what about him? If the teacher can't handle him, by God I can—"

Bertha could bear no more. "If you'd shet your big mouth a minute I'd tell you!" she shouted. "It ain't nothin' wrong about Clance I got to tell you—" she hesitated almost imperceptibly as Clarence, noiselessly and without attracting his father's notice, slunk from the room—"it's somethin' good! The teacher says he's got talent with his fiddle, he ort to go on to high school in town and learn—"

Tim's upper lip lifted in the familiar cruel smile, his yellow fangs bared to the gums. "Well, well, now ain't that jest simply grand!" he mocked her mincingly. "Got talent with his fiddle, has he? Farmin' ain't good enough fer him." He purred. "Well, I think I can fix that there all right." He began to unbuckle his belt. Bertha saw what she had done. She sprang from her chair. "Tim! You listen here! You listen here to me! It ain't Clance's fault, it's mine! You let him alone! If you got to hit somebody, go on and hit me!"

Tim grinned. "I don't hit no woman," he drawled softly. "I don't have to. I jest entertain 'em." He noticed for the first time that Clarence had gone, and abandoned his purr for a snarl of feral rage. "Where's that yeller pup at? By God, I'll learn 'im—"

He jerked the belt from his trousers and strode from the room. Bertha closed her eyes. She could not hope that Clarence would escape. His stubborn pride would keep him from running far. The next moment her certainty was confirmed; she heard Tim's bellow and the first hard blow. There was no outcry. Clarence would make none. Bertha, her hands clenched, all life suspended in her while it lasted, rocked back and forth in her chair to the ghastly rhythm of the merciless flogging, her body and mind one flame of murderous hate.... oh God, oh God, oh God, would he never stop?

I'll kill him, I'll kill him as sure as you're born, some day....
oh Clance Clance Clance, no wonder you hate me, no
wonder! She could not weep, she had no eyes to weep with,
no eyes to see. She was only flesh, her flesh and Clarence's,
beaten.

The other children watched her curiously. They were so
accustomed to Tim's brutality that they had no feeling other
than personal relief, that this time it was Clarence and not
they. Maw always taken it harder when it was Clance.

It was over. She opened her eyes. "Shet up!" she cried
violently, though none of them had spoken. "Git up and git
out o' here, ever' last one of you!"

When they had fled, she rose mechanically. Mechanically
she began to pick up the supper dishes; but when she heard
her husband come swaggering in, she set them down again
and left the house. She could not look at him, or Clarence,
tonight. She plunged through the front door into the sultry
night, still in her kitchen apron, and struck for the road, not
knowing or caring whither she went or how. Her thoughts
still moved in fragmentary rhythm: No rain, no rain, it's hot,
it's hot, it's hot. God Almighty, how hot.

Another had found it too hot for him indoors. At the Bend
she encountered the teacher, walking alone. She tried to
command her features to a smile. Her face broke. Jeff's own
smile died, and he hurried to meet her. "What is it, Bertha?
What's the matter?"

His gentleness stabbed her as nothing else could have
done. "Nothin'," she tried to say, but it was a gasp. She
turned away from him to hide her eyes. "Tim's been beatin'
up on Clance agin, that's all."

"Again? You mean—" He put his hand on her shoulder.
"Bertha, I'm sorry. What had Clance been up to?"

"He hadn't done nothin', Mr. Plant—not a livin' thing. I
done it. I ain't got the sense of a bedbug. No wonder he hates
me—"

"Who, Clance? Clance hates you? Don't be silly, Bertha.
Tell me. What was it?"

She twitched away from the comforting hand on her

shoulder. In her frenzy of self-detestation she could not bear it. "It was me, I told you I ain't got no sense! I tried to talk to Tim about the fiddlin'—"

"Oh." He put his hand again on her arm. "Bertha, my God, I'm sorry I said anything! If I'd had any idea of this—"

"It ain't your fault, Mr. Plant. Nor Clance's neither. I ain't fitten to be a mother to a sick cat. You didn't know about it, but I knowed. I jest ain't got no sense, I tell you, that's all!" She sobbed aloud.

"Come over here and sit down on this stump a minute," said Plant. "You're all out of breath. That's better. Now rest a while." He sat down beside her, took out his pipe and lighted it. "I guess it's no use going at it that way, then."

Bertha made a muffled sound. "I already knowed it."

"I wish I'd known it too. I ought to have found out. It's as much my fault as yours."

"No, it ain't," said Bertha desperately. "You wanted to help him—"

"A person can want to help and still be stupid. You wanted to help him too, you know. So if you haven't any sense at all, that makes two of us—and a bright prospect for Clance, poor little devil!"

Bertha was somewhat comforted; she stopped gasping and began to breathe. Plant was not looking at her; he held the bowl of his pipe in his cupped hand, scowling at it. "Teaching can be the devil of a job. I took a course in it once." He laughed bitterly and sharply. "Age level, grade level, normal curve of achievement. Graphs. Statistics. Lesson plans. Procedure. Very fancy course. Covered just about everything—except Clance."

Bertha was silent, not comprehending. He was not talking to her anyway, she could see.

"Everything but Clance and the teacher's involvement. Everything but the risk of playing God, and having none of God's equipment to do it with. Everything but the risk of starting a fire that never can be put out this side of hell." He let the hand drop, holding the pipe, to his knee. "You know, Bertha, sometimes I think Weary Water's right. It's a woman's job. Male or female, a teacher that cares about teaching is like an old hen—can't rest satisfied without scooping the last squalling chicken under shelter. It's a strain. Women are stronger than men, they stand up to it better."

Bertha stared at him. Women stronger than men—what kind of talk was this? Was it a man who had said this preposterous thing? Of all his words, these only she could even half understand, and these she could not believe that she had heard.

"I don't see how they stand it, bearing children," Jeff went on, more to himself than to Bertha. "It isn't as though the children were theirs to keep. They're not. First you have them torn out of your bodies, and then, almost before you know it, right out of your lives. I swear I don't see how you manage it, Bertha."

The thought of Clarence struck Bertha like a blow. A second and terrible weaning, then..... It was true. She knew he had spoken the truth. She would lose Clarence.

"Women know in their bodies and bones," he went on, "what a man knows only by reason, which isn't knowledge. They must know they are just the husk when the seed has gone. And with every child not once but over again. I think it's stupendous, Bertha, nothing less."

He fell silent, smoking. Bertha was ill at ease. She wanted to answer him, but she had no words. Much of what he had said was beyond her, but this last—"You ain't got no young 'uns of your own, have you, Mr. Plant?" she asked hesitantly.

He looked at her, surprised. "Why, no. I'm not married, Bertha. I thought you knew that."

Bertha hesitated. "Mis' Bartlett said you wasn't, but that there picture—"

He smiled. "That's just a girl I know. We're not engaged. Lovely thing, isn't she?"

Bertha did not answer. The moon seemed to her to move suddenly, illuminating his face. He was still smiling, but his smile had changed; it turned her heart over and troubled her throat to see it. Bertha had known ardor—of a kind—lust, lechery and leers, and the rude bucolic badinage that attended the daily life of the only men and women she knew, but tenderness, except from herself toward Clarence, she had never known. That a man could think of a woman and look as Jeff did strained her heart almost to bursting with envy and longing. The thought of his marrying that girl in the picture stabbed her with anguish. "She ain't half good enough fer him," her whole being protested. "She ain't got no *right*—"

"Some day I'll tell you all about it," said Jeff, "but not now. It's late. Listen." He rose to look down the road. "Somebody's coming. It's Bud—I know his whistle. Maybe you'd better—"

"Yes," answered Bertha, and crossed the road at once. In the turmoil of her thoughts Bud Wilkerson had no place, but she acted automatically, from long habit, knowing it would never do to be caught out in the dark with a man not her husband. Blindly, all her misery returning upon her, she took the direction opposite to her home and plodded toward the cheerful approaching whistle. Bud, catching sight of her, hailed her hopefully, but she made pretense of seeing and hearing nothing, and they passed. Behind her, after a moment, she heard him greeting Plant. He might put two and two together, of course, but intelligence was not Bud's strongest point and no doubt Mr. Plant would be able to fool him. It didn't matter anyhow. Nothing mattered.

She sat down again on a log by the roadside to wait. She'd never get home if she walked too far away. In the thick woods behind her the cicadas grated endlessly against the silence. A toad or a lizard disturbed the grass at her feet. The moon swung free of a bank of floating cloud, bringing out a lacework of shadows from the tall weeds around her and striping the rutted road with silver and grey. There was beauty in the night, in spite of its heat. Involuntarily Bertha lifted one hand to her shoulder where Jeff's had lain and pressed it hard, thinking painfully of the girl in the picture, the very thought of whom had made him smile like that. The smile and the pause that followed had told her too much; she resisted it, she would not let it in. "Anyhow, I was right about him," she thought proudly. "He ain't no biggety man for all he's so smart." How kindly he had talked to her. And he had even laid his hand—that hand like no other on earth—on her shoulder. Only on her shoulder, but she felt it, suddenly and sweetly, on her breast. The shock of it brought her up standing; she uttered a faint cry. "What's the matter with me, anyhow?" she whispered to the mocking cicadas. "He's as good as married, and I got a man and six young 'uns! What kind of a woman am I, anyhow?"

The cicadas answered her harshly, and so did shame. There was nothing in Bertha's life that forgave such a thought, and she felt branded by it so that any casual passerby could see the mark. "I can't never let him see me no more," she thought desolately. "He could tell it on me—anybody could." She tried to go back and unthink the thing she had thought. It was useless. Here she was, married, the mother of six, and "stuck on" the teacher.

The very word "love" all her life had brought Bertha to blush, as it did every other woman of her acquaintance. The actuality she rejected at once, summarily and, she told herself, forever. It might be all right to admire Mr. Plant and look up to him for his learning, but only a bad woman would go further than that. Bertha told herself peremptorily that she would not, but the words were meaningless. What was the use of that, when every time she commanded herself the stabbing sweetness returned upon her again?

She turned wearily and hopelessly toward home. "I'm jest naturally no-count and triflin', I reckon," she thought. "Here the other night it was Bud Wilkerson I was a-wantin'." But she knew that this was not at all like the other. She had "wanted" Bud Wilkerson only because she loathed Tim. At the thought of Jeff Plant with his arms around her—Bertha shivered—Tim disappeared from existence. "He wouldn't make no more difference than a June-bug," she thought, and was momentarily surprised—Tim, who spread through her life like a dark stain or a foul odor! But it was true.

Her whole body ached, and she was so tired she could barely walk. Arrived at last at the farm, she found the house dark; they had all gone to bed, and she could hear Tim snoring. She undressed in the dark and lay down a moment beside him. He turned over, still asleep, and his shoulder met hers. She recoiled from the contact and, suddenly attacked by nausea, plunged from the bed to the open front door and was violently sick. She did not return, but sat on the doorstep till morning.

VII

The equinoctial rains in late September began the cooling of the swamp, and October set in bright and clear and comforting. It was still warm, but mere existence was no longer so heavy a burden. The people stirred again into life and sporadic activity. Women made fitful feints at cleaning up their houses and their children; there was a singing bee at the little shingled church, and talk had been set going about a revival. It was not the time of year for one, but report had it that Sister Cory Plummer was feverishly active in nearby settlements and that Brother Pointer had been stirred to emulation. "He knows it's him or Sister Cory fer it," was the consensus at Boney Bartlett's store. "Sister Cory'll be down here next, a-rairin' and a-prancin', if he don't git in ahead of her."

The topic was endlessly discussed, not only by the tobacco-chewing senate at the store but by the women, their soggy babies perched on their sagging hips, chatting across fences. "I reckon Brother Pointer aims to have him another haul at Mamie Johnson," one of them might suggest slyly, with a cackle of excited laughter.

It was still permissible to laugh, for the revival had not begun. Later, when the meetings were in swing and the awful power of the Spirit had taken control, there would be no laughing at such as Mamie Johnson, but only a thrilled delight, half horror, at seeing her dangled over the pit of hell. It was their only revenge upon her for her shameless flouting of their standards, her libidinous ease in the face of their drudgery, and her defiant house, decked wide with the spoils of sin. "I reckon she'll wisht she had more'n a lace curtain to cover her when Brother Pointer starts a-shakin' his finger at her," a woman said with a gloating, snaggle-toothed grin. "Brother Pointer shore is a mighty man in the Sperrit when he gits a-goin' good."

"I'd sooner listen to Sister Cory, though," another said discontentedly. "Last Brother Pointer's meetin' they wasn't nobody went into a single transt the whole two weeks. Sister Cory, she put Matt Barlow's Jinny in a transt lasted all that night and a good part o' the next day. And Jin shorely come through a-buckin' when she did come."

Bertha Mallory, though she was present, contributed nothing to the conversation. She had attended none of Sister Cory's meetings as yet and had not seen Jinny Barlow, a child of Opal's age, go into her famous trance. But she had seen others as dramatic, and she did not like them. "I don't believe them transts is healthy fer young 'uns," she thought. "I'd jest like to know what Mr. Plant thinks about 'em."

She could not remember his name without a pang. At first, after that moment of searing self-revelation by the roadside, she had avoided him; if she approached the store and he went in before her, she walked on past and killed time until he came out. She never rode Jess past the schoolhouse or his dwelling, and she sent Woodrow to return his books. But with the books gone and no others to take their place, and without even the crumb of his occasional companionship to feed her gnawing hunger, she found life desolate indeed; and after a surprise encounter with him in the store, during which her first deep confusion was eased by his acting toward her exactly as he always had, she decided gratefully that he had not guessed her secret. Complete isolation was uncalled for—"as long as I tend to my own fool business," she thought bitterly.

In a few more weeks she had read several of Dickens' novels and had tried a sprinkling of other authors, with varying success. He had once given her Kipling's *Plain Tales from the Hills*, but she found these, with their casual prodigality of foreign allusions, far too difficult.

On the other hand, and much to his surprise, she had little trouble with the richly alien Scotch dialect of Barrie and MacLaren. "It don't make so much differ'nce about the way the words is wrote," she tried to explain. "Seems like the story keeps a-tellin' you what it's talkin' about as it goes along."

He looked at her as though he were surprised. It was not the first time; she had grown accustomed to seeing him look so, but she never grew accustomed to the dangerous stirrings within her when he did. On this occasion he was silent longer than usual. "I think maybe you've got something there, Bertha," he said at last.

She did not question him. He would be thinking, no doubt, of those dim mysteries that made up so much of his strange, unnatural talk—mysteries that he seemed to think needed explaining, while everybody else accepted them as a matter of course. He was always asking "Why?" and hazarding an answer. Other people did not look for reasons. They talked of crops, of revivals, of chickens that died of the pip, of the heat or the cold or the rain or the difficulty of getting diapers clean in the muddy river water—all things you could see or hear or smell or pick up. Mr. Plant had little interest in any of these. Even when he spoke to her of Clarence, as he still did sometimes in spite of her refusal to answer, it did not seem to be Clarence as Bertha knew him, but a sort of inside Clarence she had never seen. There was comfort for her in the fact that Plant never forgot the boy, but she dared not try again to do battle for him. If she listened to the teacher, she would fight. And fighting could end in nothing but disaster.

Looking back on the ecstatic moment with Clarence that

had betrayed her, she shuddered to the bone. "Jest because he let me hold him a minute," she railed inwardly, "I taken a notion I had everything all fixed up. I had it fixed up all right, now didn't I?"

She had "fixed it up" for herself as well as for Clarence. Had she restrained the impulse to speak to Tim, she might still be hugging the memory of that moment—the moment in which Clarence had spoken to her, let her touch him, flung at her—furiously, true, but unmistakably—the priceless gift of a concession to her desire. Now that sublimity was a part of horror, as dreadful to her as what had followed it. Clarence had returned to his sullen self-preoccupation, setting her as far from him as before. She knew now, with a frozen certainty, that he would have done so even without the beating; he did not hold the beating against her. He only held against her, as he had for years, the fact that she had become his mother by Tim.

She was silent, therefore, whenever Plant spoke of him; and Plant, seeing the repressed anguish in her eyes, never persisted, though she was as sure as if he had told her that he knew what her silence meant. The old fear of what Clarence's blocked and plunging emotions might do to him lay heavier upon her every day. Clance was "ornery", Mr. Plant had said, because he needed his music; the idea, totally new to Bertha, had convinced her at once. Her almost unfathomable ignorance, coupled with her quick perception and hungry intelligene, had clothed the schoolmaster in cabalistic garments. She saw him half a wizard, half an angel. She would have liked, had she known how, to talk with him about herself, her own "orneriness." She had not a moment's doubt that he could tell her whatever she wanted to know about anything—why she had married Tim Mallory in the first place, why she could not love her other children as she loved Clarence, why a man and a woman could not be friends, why a man named Dickens could take all life in his hands and put it between the covers of a book and a woman like herself could not even speak her thoughts.

That there was something lacking about her she knew

well. The "orneriness" that turned her coldly aside from Daisy and Woodrow, that made her hate the very sight and sound of Tim, that all but broke her with fury at the sight of the neighbor women's passivity in subjection, that made her scrub and scour the dingy farmhouse as though it were loaded with unspeakable filth—it must mean something, some need, some unsatisfied thing. She did not really care about the house. It was not really to keep her floors and windows clean, her children clean and healthy, that she roughened her hands and blinded her eyes with toil. It kept her from murdering Tim, perhaps, that was all.

But she could not ask the teacher what it meant. She could ask him nothing except about the books. On this ground she was safe, and on this alone. She was instantly nervous when he stepped beyond it. One day he had said to her, smiling, "You're my safety valve. I really don't know what I'd do without you, Bertha."

He meant nothing by it, she knew, but his usual kindness. Yet the sound of the words, and his open, friendly gaze, wounded her to the heart. "He can talk thataway," she thought with a flash of perception, "jest *because* he don't mean nothin' by it. That ain't the way he'd talk to that woman in there." Her heart swelled, and she had to blink back tears. They were tears of anger, for how could he be so blind? He knew everything else, why didn't he see what ailed her? Why couldn't he put his hand on her shoulder again, and say, in that kind voice of his, "I know, I know how it is. It's too bad. I'm sorry." That, she told herself fiercely, was all she wanted—just to have him know how she felt about him! "I reckon he's skeered of me," she tried to think, with contempt; but it was not so, and she knew it. He might indeed have been "skeered", and not without reason, had he rightly and fully interpreted her trouble. But nothing was plainer than his ignorance of it; had he had the least intimation, he could not have looked at her with that clear, comradely gaze.

Her anger sank down into a stoic acceptance. She knew, vaguely, that it was a manic thing. For weeks she had shunned the sight of him lest he see his own brand on her shoulder, and now she was angry with him that he did not. "Seems like everything in the world is all mixed up," Bertha told herself hopelessly. "God must be gittin' old, like Doc Brumbaugh says."

Things were mixed up indeed with Bertha at the moment. She had now not only Clarence but Opal to harass her. The talk of the revival and Mamie Johnson brought Opal's problem acutely to life within her. A new young man had come to live at Mamie's, a boy who, according to Mamie's account, was her nephew, Hughie Conroy from Gray's Mills.

Hughie was decidedly a "pretty feller" by the standards of the community. He was about seventeen, tall and powerfully built, with nostrils wide and flaring as a stallion's, and a handsome, empty head thatched with yellow curls. His mere appearance cut a swath before him, and not only in Milltown either. The Weary Water girls were mad about him.

Hughie did chores for this farmer and that, and helped in the fields, and pitched horseshoes with the men occasionally behind the store. Wherever he went a knot of giggling girls, their lips moist, their raw scaly fingers eternally pushing and patting at their own and each other's hair, went with him.

Bertha, meeting him thus attended in the store, went home grim with apprehension to lecture Opal in advance. "You jest let me ketch you follerin' him around and hangin' after him like them other little fools," she concluded at length, "and you'll shore wisht you hadn't. If you won't listen to me, I'll have somethin' to say to your daddy."

Opal, at the mirror as usual, smirked with self-satisfaction. She had a shot in her locker. "I might have somethin' to say to Paw myself," she retorted, "about all them books Daise says you keep a-gittin' from Mr. Plant." Opal was far too busy with her own affairs to do much with domestic research, but Daisy was a mine of valuable data if shrewdly approached.

Bertha rose menacingly. "What's that you say?"

"Nothin'," Opal backtracked swiftly. "Aw, what's the

matter with you, Maw, anyways? I ain't a-goin' to run after no feller, Hughie Conroy nor nobody else." She tossed her head and turned back to the mirror.

"Who told you Hughie Conroy was his name?" Bertha demanded.

Opal flung the brush down on the wash stand. "Mame Johnson did, if you want to know." At the instant and dreadful whitening of her mother's face she shrank back in alarm. "I couldn't help it, Maw, honest I couldn't. I was a-comin' outen the store door, and she stopped me and—"

"Git out o' my way," said Bertha briefly, starting for the door.

"Maw!" Opal caught at her, futilely. "Maw, where you goin'? What you goin' to do? Maw!"

Bertha made no answer. All the blood in her body seemed to have flown to the top of her head, roaring. She thrust Opal aside and left the house. Although she walked swiftly, it seemed to her that her feet would not bear her forward; Milltown, a red dazzle in her brain, receded farther from her with every step she took. To get to Milltown—only to get to Milltown and find Mamie Johnson.......

Passing the schoolhouse, she saw Jeff locking the door. She quickened her step almost to a run, but he saw her. "Bertha! Wait a minute!" he shouted. "I want to ask you—"

She halted, seething. He was always around. Every time she started anywhere she met him. She wanted to ignore his call, but she could not. He caught up with her, noticed her pallor and the mingled fury and fear in her eyes, and stopped short. "Bertha! What's the matter now? Where are you going?" He caught her arm.

"I'm a-goin' to Milltown. Lemme go, Mr. Plant. Lemme go! I ain't got no time to lose!"

"Clarence?"

"No, it ain't Clarence. It's Opal. Mame Johnson, she tried to sic Opal onto that there boy she's got livin' with her. Opal don't need no sickin' in no sech direction. I have to watch ever' move she makes as it is." She tried to pull her arm away. "Lemme go!"

He held her. "To see Mamie Johnson? You won't help
Opal that way. Why, good God, Bertha, you ought to know
that! The whole place'll be buzzing with it in no time.
Everybody'll think Opal's already in trouble."

"How do I know she ain't?" Bertha flung back, frantic.

"Well, Mamie Johnson can't tell you. And there's nothing
to be gained by getting Opal talked about, you know that.
Once let them get a girl's name in their gabbing mouths and
she might as well have the game and be done with it. Opal's
nothing but a child, anyway; what's the matter with you,
Bertha? You're imagining things."

Bertha shook her head. "Opal ain't no child, Mr. Plant.
Don't you believe it. Opal knows what she's a-doin', well
and good. I ain't never saw no girl in these parts was a child
after she was twelve years old. Lots of 'em's married by
then."

"They're still children," Plant said patiently. "Listen,
Bertha, the thing for you to do is tackle this at the other end.
Forget Mamie. Opal's the one for you to talk to. I think
you're out of your head. I see Opal every day at school, and I
haven't noticed anything out of the way. What makes you
think she's headed for trouble?"

"Opal's *borned* fer trouble," Bertha replied doggedly.

"Nonsense, Bertha. You know better than that."

She was silent, but she left him persuade her gradually to
turn back, for she knew that what he had said about neighborhood gossip was true. Did anyone so much as suspect
that she had gone to Milltown to "jump" Mamie Johnson
about her daughter, Opal's reputation was as good as
ruined.

It seemed incredible now that she had not seen this for
herself, that Mr. Plant had had to point it out. "I reckon it's a
right good thing I run into him this time," she thought
dully as she plodded home.

Her elbow ached from the tightening grasp with which he
had held her. There was a certain pleasure in the pain,
though this had been violence and not compassion. Nothing
but violence, she knew, she could have restrained her. She

had been beside herself, she had had black murder in her heart.

Half unconsciously she noticed Brother Pointer, walking across a field with Molly at his heels. She remembered the revival. Every night—she would see Mr. Plant every night, at least for a while; and she would not have to try to talk to him. She could just sit there and watch him playing the organ. The thought of Opal receded from her mind. She stood still in the road for a moment and glanced about her, as though looking for something; then, recalling herself, she trudged on back to the farm.

VIII

Nobody thought it odd that Mamie Johnson should come, year after year and several times a year, to hear herself publicly reprehended first by Brother Pointer and then by Sister Cory Plummer, while her neighbors gazed in fascination at her lace stockings, her great pearl bead earrings, her tight near-satin dresses, and her lavish make-up. Except for Dr. Brumbaugh, whose attendance was sporadic, every man, woman and child in Weary Water went to every meeting of every revival, the only deterrent being actual inability to move or be moved. Mamie not only attended but, apparently, enjoyed herself.

The other citizens gave her a wide berth, but she sat bland and imperturbable though alone, Hughie preferring the noisy society of other young bucks at the back of the room, and chewed her peppermint gum with placid vigor throughout. She was a woman of a good deal of natural color, having sharp black eyes and abundant eyebrows. She had long ago discovered peroxide, and some striking ensembles had resulted, but she had never achieved such a coiffure as that with which she celebrated the opening of the new revival.

revival. Mamie was nothing if not receptive to new ideas. The arrival of Bertha Mallory in Weary Water had stimulated her imagination, and she now appeared with hair of an explosive henna tint that rocked the other women to their foundations.

It rocked Brother Pointer, too. He stared at it, his mild features working. "Is the teacher here, or anybody that'll play fer us?" he managed to say at last, wrenching his eyes from Mamie with an effort.

Jeff Plant rose from his seat beside the Wilkersons and made his way forward to the rheumatic reed organ that stood near the pulpit. He twirled the stool a time or two and sat down, waiting. "We'll sing number sixty-nine, Mr. Plant, if you please," Brother Pointer said hurriedly.

Jeff opened the organ hymnal, laid his long fingers on the keys and pressed the pedals. The organ emitted a roupy little bleat, as if to clear its throat, and conversation died away. The singing rose, lustily:

> *As I went on to sing and shout*
> *I found an inward foe;*
> *The Holy Spirit burnt him out;*
> *Praise the Lord.... it's so!*

"Ay—men!" contributed Bud Wilkerson jovially, looking past his Lucy at Bertha Mallory and deliberately winking. Bud always began a revival in a state of high jocularity, growing soberer and soberer as the meetings went on and the Spirit came pushing and prodding him toward conviction. He was merry tonight, and had begun patting his foot with the very first line of the hymn.

Bertha looked the other way. She was not singing. She never sang in church. She sat between Daisy and the glowering Clarence, with Ardeth nestling in her lap and sucking a piece of bright pink wintergreen candy. Tim, his pepper-and-salt hair combed into a stiff upstanding brush, was keeping a minatory eye on Clovis and Woodrow as he sang. Opal was not with the family; she had gone to join the girls of her Sunday-school class at the back of the church. Bertha knew that she was joining them also in the daring and delicious glances they kept sending toward the opposite side, where the teen-aged boys, Hughie Conroy among them, sat chewing paper into pellets for convenient throwing.

But this, she told herself, she could not help; Young 'uns would be young 'uns, and as long as they stayed in the churchhouse not much could happen to them.

> *"Praise the Lord, it's so,*
> *Praise the Lord, it's so;*
> *The Holy Spirit burnt him out;*
> *Praise the Lord, it's so!"*

sang the congregation, ending the first hymn. Brother Pointer quickly announced another. *"There's No Disappointment in Heaven.* Number thirty. Sing, brothers and sisters, sing ye unto the Lord! Number thirty, Mr. Plant."

Jeff turned the pages, and again the music swelled forth.

> *We'll never pay rent on our mansions,*
> *The taxes will never come due;*
> *Our garments will never be threadbare,*
> *But always be fadeless and new.*
> *The clouds of our earthly horizon*
> *Will never appear in the sky.....*

Bertha sat silent, holding Ardeth, her free hand pleating and unpleating a fold of her brown cotton skirt. The oil lamps, flaring murkily against their fluted tin reflectors, cast a rich additional glow upon her glowing hair. She avoided looking at Tim, knowing that an angrily expressive jerk of his head would reprimand her silence if he caught her eye. He had "took her apart" about this matter, as usual, before they had left home. "You c'n yowl loud enough when the notion takes you. I heerd you the other day, plumb down to the river. Even the fish was skeered. How do you reckon it

makes me look, you goin' to church and jest settin' there like
a bump on a log when Brother Pointer tells the people to
sing?"

"I don't have to go to church, then," Bertha had retorted.

"You'll go to church," Tim stated succinctly, his little
eyes narrowing the crafty cruelty. "Them's some o' Clance's
fancy notions you got, thinkin' you don't have to go to
church. Ain't they?" he suddenly bellowed at her.

"No, they ain't."

"They better not be," Tim vouchsafed. "I'll take the hide
plumb offen him if I ever hear o' him gittin' sech things in
his stubborn head or puttin' 'em in yourn. You have them
young 'uns ready to go, and be ready to go yourself, time I git
back here with the wagon."

He had waited long enough for his threat to take effect,
and then left her. And here she was, boiling inwardly with
self-contempt but helpless in the power of her love for Clarence. That Tim rejoiced in any opportunity to "take out" on
Clarence the fact that his wife despised him was blatantly
apparent. It gave him a weapon as potent as his use of it was
sickening. Bertha knew the threat was not an idle one. So she
had come to church; but still she would not sing.

The comparative serenity of "There's No Disappointment in Heaven" passed quickly into the stirring, strongly
marked rhythm of "The Old Account Was Settled Long
Ago." Feet were patting now all over the room. There was a
change, a quickening, in the atmosphere. An almost palpa-
ble wave of excitement was rising; there would be no long
preliminary singing and praying tonight. A row of adoles-
cent girls a little older than Opal's group, sitting near the
platform, shuddered in unison, as though swept by a sudden
icy wind, and their shoulders began to sway rhythmically.

Without further warning the singing leapt from fervor to
ecstasy. Brother Pointer, who had been kneeling in prayer
on the platform, stood up, his nostrils dilating, his mystic's
eyes ablaze. He broke without preamble into passionate
appeal:

"Oh, my brethren, there's a hour a-comin' when the sun'll

be darkened and the moon'll drap from heaven and the stars'll be a-drippin' with blood, with blood! And how many of the sinful, how many of the sinners in this here room'll be able to stand? In that day, in that hour the Lord Christ is a-comin' with the sound of trumpets and call His own, and fer them that's left behind the mouth of hell and destruction's a-yawnin'. Look that it don't yawn fer *you*! Look that it don't yawn fer *you*! Oh, my brother, oh, my sister, He wants to save you, He waits to save you, there on the right hand of God the Father in heaven he sets and pleads with you not to put it off, not to throw away this here chanst He's a-givin' you to come and be forever saved. Saved from sin and shame, to injoy with Him the blessin's of eternal life in that glorious land over yander beyant the skies! Come, fer His hand's a-stretchin' out to save! Come, fer the shinin' path lays open before you! Come, fer you may never see the sun rise on another day—"

A sobbing woman pushed her way forward and fell on her knees beside the platform.

"That's right, sister. That's right, sister. God bless you. Christians come and pray for her. Christians come. That's right, brother—" as a gray-headed man crept forward and knelt beside the woman at the mourner's bench. "Never too late, never too late to come to Jesus, praise the Lord! Yit it's a blessed thing, a beautiful thing, to see young souls a-givin' theirselves to Him in the mornin' of their lives. And oh, my young friends—" Brother Pointer's voice cracked with the intensity of his yearning,—"if you only knowed the blessedness o' belongin' to Him and follerin' in His footsteps and doin' His will, nothin' would hold you back. Come! will you grieve Him forever, Him that hung on the bloody cross that you might be saved and live everlastin'ly in the light of His glorious kingdom?"

"Glory to God! Glory to God! He's heerd me! I'm saved! I'm saved!" shrieked the woman who had first come forward.

"Amen, dear sister! Give Him the praise!" cried Brother Pointer, his kindly face aglow with joy. "One sister has found a blessin'. Ain't there others? Ain't there others? Ain't there others here tonight that wants one too?''

They were coming forward rapidly now. Shouts and sobs arose all over the room. Around the huddled, wailing forms at the mourner's bench the Christians knelt, praying aloud, and Brother Pointer's voice rose hoarse and strained above the frenzy of other voices. A pale, wild-eyed girl screamed once and fell back, apparently lifeless, on the floor. Bertha Mallory shivered.

She looked at Jefferson Plant, who had turned half aside from the organ, his wide shoulders drooping a little, his face expressionless. "He don't like it no better'n I do," she thought.

Little Molly Pointer, bewildered and half asleep, had wandered up the aisle to the organ and laid her hand on Jeff's knee. He started, looked down at her, then drew her to his side, stroking her bright hair. Molly yawned widely and looked up at him, smiling. The two looked as detached, as completely set off in a world of their own, as though no clamoring chaos surged about them.

The first night had given earnest of the new revival's quality. The mourners' bench was crowded every evening, and every evening the prayers and exhortations mounted steadily, in both violence and volume, to an overwhelming crescendo. On the seventh night Bud Wilkerson, wearing an expression of trouble that sat oddly on his alert and mobile features, was among the first to go forward for prayer.

Bud was hard to convert. No revival ended without his making the attempt, but, although he prayed and implored until his hickory shirt was soaked with sweat and the veins stood out on his temples, he never quite "came through." Brother Pointer would stand over him, a hand on his shoulder, earnestly entreating that tonight, at last, the mercy of the Spirit might be vouchsafed him, but every meeting came to a close with Bud still prostrate and still despairingly unshriven. Lucy, her blank eyes showing the only interest she ever displayed except in the occasional scandalous gossip of the neighborhood, knelt dutifully by his side and joined her prayers with his, and Tim Mallory, an established Christian of long standing, labored pompously in his cause. None of them could help poor Bud, who had apparently—dreadful thought!—sinned away his day of grace forever.

The fervor of the evangel rode so high upon occasion as to impress even Mamie Johnson, who was seen several times to stop chewing her gum and look faintly and resentfully alarmed. Brother Pointer, who even in the midst of his exhortations never missed a signal of desire, went to her side again and again to plead with her.

"I know it ain't no easy thing fer you, Mis' Johnson. Your heart's ben hardened against your Saviour's love. The human heart gits awful hard in sin. But oh, if you only knowed what peace, what blessin' would be yourn! Won't you come tonight? Won't you let me lead you forrerd here tonight, out of the mud and mire of sin and into the glorious light of His presence and forgiveness?"

Mamie would not. At his every approach her jaws began to move again, and she listened in stolid silence, chewing her gum. When he had given up and gone away she hitched herself erect in her seat, preening the froth of shoddy lace that covered her bosom. If he had been especially urgent, she took a pot of rouge out of her purse and repaired her gaudy make-up.

Bertha, in spite of her distrust of revivals, could not help hoping that Opal would be moved this time to go forward. When she could do so without being noticed by Tim, she turned her head to catch a glimpse of her daughter. But she found Opal always oblivious to the praying, her active, deeply shadowed blue eyes seeking first one and then another of the boys across the aisle.

Clarence sat scowling nightly by his mother's side, in an atmosphere thick with inarticulate rage. "God-derned fools," she heard him mutter once.

The words comforted rather than distressed her. She had no desire for Clarence's salvation as salvation was understood here. To see him broken and bent, lying abjectly across the mourners' bench beneath the bludgeoning of the accusing Spirit, was a thing she blindly felt she could not have borne. "I reckon I don't need to worry none about that," she thought with grim satisfaction. "Clance ain't a-beggin' fer nothin' from nobody, not him."

The impropriety of this sentiment was quite clear to Bertha. God had struck people dead for less, she knew. Rejoicing, nevertheless, fled along her veins at the thought, together with a possessive pride in the boy's tough single resistance.

What would happen, she wondered, if Tim tried to force him to go forward? This idea at first turned her cold with apprehension, but after a moment her fear left her. "Brother Pointer wouldn't have it," she consoled herself, with a sudden respect for the old preacher's integrity. "He ain't a wantin' no souls that don't want to come forward on their own hook."

IX

Two days before the end of the revival Ardeth was smitten with a sharp fever, and Bertha, perforce, remained at home to take care of her. The rest of the family went to the meeting as usual.

"Is she bad, Doc?" Bertha asked fearfully, a superstitious dread of retribution upon her.

Dr. Brumbaugh straightened himself, rising from the side of the bed on which the child lay. "Pretty bad, I'm afraid," he said. "It's her stomach—ptomaine poisoning. She must have picked up some trash somewhere and eaten it." He snapped his black case shut. "We'll pull her through, though, I reckon. At any rate"—he looked approvingly about him at the immaculate house, the snowy bed-clothing—"she won't have to fight the filth most of the young 'uns around here have to contend with. You're a good housekeeper, Mrs. Mallory."

Bertha drew a shuddering breath of relief. "Must I give her that medicine all night tonight?"

"Tonight and tomorrow night, yes. After that I hope it won't be necessary." The doctor turned toward the door. "I'll come in and see her again tomorrow. If she's no better,

81

I'll get Jennings to come out from town. Don't worry, Mrs. Mallory. We'll pull her through."

Bertha sat by the child's bedside all that night, trying to read, in the intervals of active attendance, the latest book Jeff Plant had given her. But she could not focus her eyes on its close-woven print. What kind of a mother was she, what kind of a woman, when her first thought in the face of Ardeth's danger was for herself and the torments of remorse she knew she would suffer if the child died?

She scarcely heard the others when they came in. Her merciless thoughts plunged on, leading her deeper and deeper into self-condemnation. She ought to love Ardeth as much as she loved Clarence, she knew. But what if she didn't and couldn't? "There ain't nothin' there to feel no sech a way about," she thought despairingly. "S'posin' she did die, she'd jest be better off, with a daddy like Tim—and a mammy like me!" she added searingly.

She could not feel the same, at all, about Clarence. Not only her own overpowering love for him but a sense of something beside, something she knew no way to define, told her that she must not let anything happen to Clarence. She could not shield him from suffering, but she would keep him alive and struggling whatever it cost her. She would fight God single-handed, if necessary, to keep him alive.

Ardeth was no worse next day, though not perceptibly better either. Dr. Brumbaugh decided to wait another day before calling in outside help. "She's holding her own," he said reassuringly.

Bertha settled herself for another night of vigil. At ten o'clock there was a scuffle outside the door, and Clarence, first looking in warily to make sure his father had not preceded him, disappeared and reappeared in a moment, thrusting a struggling and terrified Opal before him.

"I brung her home," he panted to his mother. "You better watch her. I ketched her a-goin' off in the woods with that there Hughie Conroy." He clapped a hand suddenly against his mouth. "I bloodied his god-derned nose fer him oncet in his life, anyhow."

"Yeah—you think you're so smart!" snapped Opal, gasping. "Look at your own!" She turned apprehensively to Bertha. "I wasn't doin' nothin', Maw—we was jest—"

"Hesh your mouth," Bertha said, "or you'll wake up Ardeth."

She lifted the lamp from the table and held it nearer them. It was only too evident that Clarence had been no match for the muscular Hughie. One of his eyes was swollen shut, his shirt sleeve was torn its full length, his knuckles were badly skinned, and blood from his nose and mouth streaked his face and his clothing.

Bertha turned on Opal. "You march yourself straight off to bed, young lady," she commanded. "I'll talk to you in the mornin'." She turned to Clarence. "How'd you git away from your daddy?" she demanded.

"Him and Bud Wilkerson was a-talkin'," Clarence responded, again pressing his hand to his mouth.

"Well, come on in the kitchen and let me wash that there blood offen your face before he gits here." Bertha set the lamp down, but Clarence had already started toward the kitchen. "I'll wash it off my own self," he growled. "You better watch that derned little fool; she ain't got the sense she was borned with."

He began to splash furiously in the kitchen wash basin, and Bertha, sick with double fear of what might have happened—might still happen—to Opal and what would almost certainly happen to Clarence if Tim noticed his swollen eye, sat down again beside the bed, a line of cold sweat on her upper lip, her bosom rising and falling rapidly. She must not give way to weakness. She must think, and think fast.

She forced herself to her feet, her knees buckling under her, and went into the kitchen. "Clance," she said hurriedly, leaning on the table for support, "you hurry up and git out o' here before your daddy comes in. You don't want him to see that there eye till the swellin's went down a little."

Clarence did not indeed. He took his face out of the roller towel and looked at her blankly.

"Where'd I go?" he said. He had not thought until now, apparently, of his own peril, and the quick terror in his eyes sickened her anew. "There ain't no place to go to."

"Yes, there is. You go down to Mr. Plant's. He'll let you stay all night. Maybe he'll know somethin' to do fer your eye that'll make it look better."

"I got to come home some time," Clarence pointed out doggedly.

"Not till after school tomorrow. Maybe it'll be better by then."

"What you goin' to tell *him*?" Clarence jerked his head toward the open door, through which at any moment Tim might come.

"I'll fix him. I'll tell him Mr. Plant wasn't feelin' good and ast me to let you come. Hurry up. There ain't no time to stand here a-foolin'."

Clarence hesitated but a moment. He dropped the towel and went. Just outside the door he paused a moment, retching; but as she came swiftly after him to hold his head he straightened himself, with an inarticulate sound, and plunged toward the gate.

Bertha returned to the sickroom, forcing herself into a stony calm. Somehow she could do it. Somehow she made her hands stop trembling, made herself sit down. She even remembered to hide, under Ardeth's bedclothing, the book she had been trying to read earlier in the evening.

Tim and Daisy and the twins arrived almost at once, and she told her merciful lie without a quiver, icily disregarding the objurgations with which her husband received it.

"It looks mighty funny to me," Tim pronounced, his gimlet eyes boring into her, "that a growed-up man like Mr. Plant'd send fer a squirt of a boy to look after him. Why'n't he send fer Doc Brumbaugh if he's sick? He's thick enough with Brumbaugh, infidel or no infidel."

"He knowed Doc Brumbaugh was here with Ardeth." Bertha had not intended to tell this second lie, and the sound of the words appalled her; suppose Dr. Brumbaugh had been at the revival? She glanced in apprehension toward Daisy, who as usual stood listening, nibbling reflectively at her nails.

But apparently Dr. Brumbaugh had not been at the revival, for neither Daisy nor Tim intimated as much. Tim sent the children peremptorily to bed and sat down in a rickety rocker, his little dark eyes following Bertha as she moved about the bed making things comfortable for the sleeping Ardeth. The hostility and suspicion in his gaze were veiled by something else, and he wet his lips repeatedly with his tongue.

Bertha knew what these things meant. Tim, excited by the furor of the revival and still wakeful in spite of the unaccustomed lateness of the hour, was eying her with ardor—of a kind. There was one sure way in which she could conciliate him—there was always one sure way—

Her muscles stiffened with loathing. But it was for Clarence. He had only until after school tomorrow to make his eye presentable. He would probably not be able to do it. If she could put Tim in a good humor now, tonight, it might last—it sometimes did—long enough to enable the boy to escape him.

Wildly, and for no recognizable reason, she thought of Jefferson Plant.

Tim got up from his chair, restlessly, sat down, and got up again. "Don't you never comb that hair o' yourn?" he yapped at her suddenly, his eyes, moist with longing, upon it. "You look like a frizzled chicken. You put me in mind o' Mamie Johnson."

For answer Bertha, with two quick motions, snatched the pins from her hair. It fell about her, shining, and he seized her.

Opal, next morning, was duly taken to task. "Ain't you ashamed of yourself?" Bertha began. "A pretty-lookin' thing you was, comin' home last night with your hair lookin' like a frizzled chicken"—a stab of revulsion pierced her as she uttered the reminiscent words—"and Clance a-havin' to drag you every step o' the way? It ain't nothin' to you, I reckon, to git your brother in Dutch with his daddy a-takin' keer of a girl that ain't got sense enough to take keer of herself!"

"No, it ain't," Opal interrupted pertly. "Clance thinks he's so all-fired smart, I jest hope Paw does—"

"Hesh up." Bertha glared at her. "I ought to know you good enough by now, I reckon, to know you'd never give a livin' thought to nobody but yourself. But you let me tell you right now, young lady, it's yourself you better be thinkin' of and no more foolin' about it. I feel like takin' you acrost my knee and givin' you a whippin' you'd remember till the day you die. But it wouldn't do no good, I reckon."

"Y' right there, anyhow," Opal retorted. "It wouldn't."

"No smart talk outen you, my lady, or I'll take a chanst on it anyhow. I'll plumb take the hide offen you. Stringin' off to the woods with that there Hughie Conroy! A boy that lives with a bad woman!"

"It ain't Hughie's fault if Mamie Johnson's a bad woman, is it?" whined Opal. "Hughie he—"

"Whether it is or whether it ain't, you keep away from him, do you hear me? You push me too far and I'll let your daddy settle your case. I reckon when he gits done with you you won't be wantin' to go off to the woods with nobody."

But this, Bertha well knew, was an empty threat. Nothing would have induced her to turn any of the children over to Tim for punishment. She herself punished them, in the only ways she knew, when she felt herself driven past endurance, but she did not enjoy it; it left her weak and miserable for hours. Tim's sadistic relish added to this pain was far too much to bring upon herself, even if any constructive purpose would be served, which was doubtful.

In Opal's present case, certainly, no punishment would be effective. Something else was called for, and how was she to know what it was? "You talk to her," Jefferson Plant had advised. But how were you to talk to a girl who sulked to your face and, the minute your back was turned, smirked in vindictive triumph at your helplessness?

Her threat of Tim had weakened her attack past recovery.

With another word or two she let Opal go and returned to Ardeth's bedside. Opal flounced away, untroubled. A few minutes later her mother heard her fussing and fuming at her hair before the kitchen mirror.

Ardeth was better, Dr. Brumbaugh said when he arrived early in the afternoon. "Keep her in bed awhile yet, though," he added, "and give her these drops every four hours or so. Here's some oranges Mr. Plant sent her. He went to town last night." He took six oranges serially from his sagging pockets. "You better just squeeze 'em and give her the juice, I reckon."

"That was mighty nice o' Mr. Plant," Bertha said automatically as she took them. But her heart had frozen. Mr. Plant had gone to town last night. Then where had Clarence gone, and where was he now?

She listened to the doctor's parting instructions with only half her attention, and the moment he had gone she flew out the side door, looking in all directions. It was probably all right, she told herself; the afternoon session of school was not yet over. Wherever Clarence had spent the night, he was probably in school now and would be home as usual. In any event, she could not leave Ardeth alone.

She would have to hide the oranges, though, before Tim saw them. She turned back into the house, swept them into her apron and started toward the kitchen, only to be confronted with Tim coming in the side door, his face darkly flushed. "Git me a drink o' water," he ordered. "I ain't feelin' good." He slumped into a chair, his head in his hands. "Put some sody in it," he called after her as she disappeared into the kitchen. "What'st that there you got in your apron?"

Bertha murmured indistinctly in reply and made her escape, hiding the oranges temporarily in the food cupboard and returning almost at once with the water and soda. In a way, she thought, Tim's sudden indisposition was a godsend. Whether he were really ill or not, he would probably be preoccupied with himself for the rest of the day, and Clarence's battered countenance might escape notice. "Maybe you better lay down awhile," she suggested.

Tim grunted. "That's what I thought."

When he had drunk the water she helped him to bed, forcing herself to lay a testing hand on his forehead. "Looks like maybe you got a little bit o' fever," she said mendaciously.

He grunted again. "Think maybe better send fer Doc?"

"Doc jest left." She paused, considering. It would be easy enough to intercept Dr. Brumbaugh and ask him not to mention the oranges. "I'll send Daise after him if you want," she offered, "soon's she gits home from school."

Tim made no reply. Apparently he had asked for the doctor only to challenge objection. Ardeth woke and called feebly, "Maw!"

Bertha moved from one to the other, adjusting and assuaging. She was very tired; the brief confinement of Ardeth's illness had borne down upon her as no heavy prolonged labor could do. She was desperately in need of the relief of hard work, of a gallop on Jess's back over the countryside. The cool autumn air coming in through the still open windows tempted her almost beyond endurance. Since the beginning of Ardeth's attack she had not once seen the teacher, and she longed inexpressibly for some contact with him, however slight; or, if not that, at least a little time to be alone and think about him.

She shook herself impatiently. "I reckon the less o' that kind o' thinkin', the better," she thought grimly. Then, passing the window, she uttered an involuntary exclamation of joy and relief.

"What is it?" Tim demanded instantly and suspiciously.

"Nothin'." Bertha turned from the window and went about her work. "I thought they was a strange boy a-comin' acrost the yard, but it ain't. It's jest Clance."

Clarence had spent the night with Mr. Plant after all, he told her next day when she asked him. Doors were almost never locked in Weary Water, and he had simply gone in and waited until the teacher returned.

"I hope you didn't bother Mr. Plant none." Bertha threw this sop to conventionality merely in the hope of learning something about what had passed between them. "He didn't think it was funny or anything, did he?"

Clarence shook his head. "Nope. Jest said it was a good thing I come or the fire'd 'a' been plumb out."

Bertha proceeded cautiously. "I don't reckon you and him talked much, bein's he got home from town so late."

Clarence laughted shortly. "It don't never git too late fer him to talk. He ain't got no sense." He added the last five words automatically, but Bertha, who knew him better than he dreamed, was quite well aware that they expressed a certain grudging gratitude for Jeff's interest, perhaps even a little affection for Jeff himself.

Bertha hesitated. "What'd he talk about, Clance?"

The wall flew up. Clarence narrowed his eyes. "Aw, nothin' but a lot o' tommyrot, like always." He started toward the door, but glanced back over his shoulder. "All he's doin's talkin' himself outen a job, if he ain't keerful." And with this cryptic revelation he left the house. Bertha, fuming with exasperation and unsatisfied curiosity, clenched her fists in an effort to keep from shouting after him. Talking himself out of a job; now what did that mean? What could a teacher say to a boy of thirteen that would affect his job?

Late that afternoon she seized an opportunity to saddle Jess and ride past both the schoolhouse and Jeff's shack, but she was disappointed; she did not catch even a fleeting glimpse of him. Unutterably desolate in mind, she returned and got through the supper work and the dishwashing. She attended to the wants of Tim and Ardeth and, when all were in bed, sat for a long time in her rocking-chair, swaying absently back and forth and wondering what had become of Mr. Plant. "Likely he's a-settin' down there in his shack a-writin' letters to that there woman!" she thought miserably. The woman's picture rose again before her, especially the hands, the beautiful, idle and yet impressive hands clasped at the edge of a table or a desk. Bertha looked down at her own hands, strong, red and hardened with heavy work.

Suddenly she rose and tiptoed into the kitchen. She took a

bowl from the cupboard and, removing the clean white cloth from a crock of buttermilk, filled the smaller bowl half full and replaced the cover on the crock. She lifted her hands as though to plunge them into the bowl, but did not. She stood there a moment, the motion arrested midway; and then, with a muttered exclamation, she flung the milk, bowl and all, out the kitchen window.

X

No secret was long a secret in Weary Water. By this time Tim Mallory's brutality to his children was common talk. The other farmers disapproved, but not violently. The women, whose lives were so dull that any incident relieved them, expressed unbounded horror but on the whole enjoyed it. Only Bud Wilkerson was moved to rage, and when the gossip at Bartlett's store rose to a climax with the news that Tim had all but beaten Clovis to death in the middle of the south meadow he got up and paced the floor. "If'n somebody elst don't give that there Goddamned bullyin' bastard what's a-comin' to him, by God I'm a-goin' to!" he declared.

One of the other men made a cautioning gesture; Bertha had entered. Brother Pointer, who had been about to interrupt Bud and rebuke him for his profanity, greeted her nervously but kindly, "Mornin', Mis' Mallory," in an attempt to cover the embarrassing silence.

Bertha made no response beyond the curtest possible nod. She made her purchases in the midst of the silence and walked stoically out of the store. Brother Pointer, after a moment's hesitation, rose and followed her. "Mis' Mallory," he began uncertainly.

But she did not look back, she only quickened her pace. She had heard nearly every word that Bud had spoken, and she knew beyond question that he had spoken of Tim. Burning with shame, she plodded back to the farm. The day was cold and had the tang of winter, but Bertha was too hot within to know it. It wasn't enough that Tim should abuse the children, he had to make a show of it as well. He had to do it out in the open where everybody could see it and gabble about it. She knew her neighbors too thoroughly to be unaware that, except for Bud Wilkerson and Brother Pointer and the teacher, they enjoyed what they professed to reprehend.

And even those three would not do anything about it. Bertha was torn between her natural gratitude for their sympathy and her fury at their ineptitude, which was certainly greater than her own, since they were men and were not married to Tim! She could have done plenty, she told herself fiercely, but for her need to guard Clarence. "I don't reckon no man amounts to much when you git right down to it," she thought miserably.

This hopeless conclusion tinged her manner with contempt when, that afternoon, Brother Pointer timidly "looked in on her" while Tim was out, Ardeth asleep and the other children still away at school. She greeted him civilly and asked him in, but beyond that grudging concession she would not go. Having given him a chair and seated herself in another, she left the entire burden of the interview to him.

Brother Pointer's faded blue eyes were full of distress. He cleared his throat. "Mis' Mallory," he began uneasily, "or Berthy, that is, if'n you won't take it wrong in me to call you Berthy—"

"It don't make no differ'nce to me what you call me," said Bertha stonily.

Brother Pointer sighed. "We all got our troubles, you know, Mis' Mallory—Berthy." He hesitated. "I jest can't help it if I see you got yourn too. I'm afeared things is right hard fer you by times."

Bertha said nothing. He cleared his throat again. "Seemed

like to me maybe you needed somebody to help you; so I come. The Lord laid it on me to come here and see you today." He paused again, but her impassive countenance gave him no assistance. "Our dear blessed Lord, you know, Berthy, He suffered too. He was whipped till the blood run down; He was pierced with thorns! Ner they wasn't satisfied not even with that. They druv Him through with nails to that awful cross, and they left Him a-hangin' there stretched out till He died. He knows. He knows how you feel. He's a-waitin' now to help you."

Bertha laughed. Brother Pointer was grieved; he shook his head. "Don't harden your heart that way, now, Berthy. Don't you, do it. It's wrong; it'll only make things worser fer you. I know I ain't the one to help you much. I'm old and weak and full o' sin myself. I ain't got the stren'th to help you, ner the power. But He says to me there in the store, 'You're Berthy's brother'—"

"Brother!" Bertha's eyes suddenly blazed, and she laughed again. "Ain't you ashamed to have the face, and you a preacher, to say a thing like that there? They ain't no sech thing as brothers and sisters. You might be Tim's brother, maybe, but you ain't mine! You're a man, Brother Pointer, and I'm a woman. You must 'a' fergot that, I reckon, didn't you?"

He shook his head. "No, Berthy. I never fergit it. Man or woman, it don't make no differ'nce to our blessed Lord. The Good Book says male and female created He them, but it don't say man and woman can't love and help each other in the love o' Christ."

Bertha sat forward in her chair. "It don't, don't it? Then why'n't you preach it thataway? Why'n't you tell 'em it's all right to love each other? Must 'a' ben no preacher sence the Bible was wrote ever told the folks nothin' like that, the way they act! You jest try bein' a woman oncet and lovin' a man—"

She checked herself; what had she almost said? She sank sullenly back in her chair, her guilt finding relief in cruelty. "Preachers is a pretty pore lot, it look like to me."

Brother Pointer, whose eyes were not so dim as they some-times looked, inclined his white head. "Yes, Mis' Mallory, preachers is a might pore lot, take 'em all in all. It ain't no easy job to be worthy fer God." He lifted his eyes to hers. "Mis' Mallory," he added bravely and honestly, "I never knowed nary a thing about this here. I come a-thinkin' your troubles was all with Tim—"

She interrrupted him again. "I don't know's you got any call to think differ'nt now. I don't keer what you think, though. Think what you please."

He was silent and troubled for a minute or two. When he spoke at last it was plainly with difficulty. "It's laid on me. I got to say it, Berthy. It's laid on me to tell you; I can't help it." He took out a shabby blue bandanna and passed it over his trembling features. "Sometimes we think we want some-thin' that ain't ourn. They ain't no good can ever come o' that there. I know what I'm a-talkin' about. I done it." He passed an unsteady hand through his hair and sighed. "They ain't no sin I ain't committed in my heart, and they ain't many I ain't committed in my flesh. I ben through it all; I know how it is. It looks mighty nice to us whilst we're a-yearnin' fer it. It seems like we're burnin' up inside with-out it. But we ain't, Berthy. He loves us. He won't let us."

"I never seen no signs that He loved me much," said Bertha airily.

"No, Berthy, o'course you never. Your pore eyes is sealed. They was a time I couldn't see it neither. I couldn't see nothin' but the thing I wanted. It was Him that come to me and lifted me up, and opened my eyes to His everlastin' glory. And when I seen that, Berthy, I knowed, I knowed! I seen that all human love was nothin' aside o' His'n. I seen it was nothin' aside o' the terrible crystal, aside o' the sons o' the mornin' a-shoutin' fer joy!"

He waited, but she did not answer him. He tried again.

"I looked in my heart, and I seen what a mess it was. All wantin' and yearnin' and fumin' and frettin' and pain. You look in your heart now, Berthy, and look in it honest—they's somethin' back there a-tryin' to hide in the dark. You think

it's a brother you want, but it ain't no brother. If'n it was, I'd
'do jest as well as anybody else. Yes, old and wore out and
broke down as I am, I'd do. But a brother's love'd be all I had
to give you; and that you don't want, fer you tole me so
before."

In the face of this dire truth-telling Bertha was silent.
Brother Pointer went on, his tone a little changed. "Don't
fergit, Berthy, they's more in it than you. I know what it is to
love wrong; it's a terrible thing. It stands in the way of us
gittin' to know our Lord, and more'n that, it makes us fergit
other things we ort to remember—"

"You jest this minute said a man and a woman—"

"In the love o' Christ it don't make no differ'nce, Berthy.
But jest in the love o' Christ, not no other way. It ain't the
love o' Christ that brings a man and a woman together when
they ain't each other's. It turns 'em against their own. You
got six children—"

Bertha, flicked on her sorest secret wound, became flip-
pant. "Now ain't it funny I never thought to count 'em!"

Brother Pointer looked at her directly. "Oncet in a while,
Berthy," he told her, "it does look right funny to me."

Bertha flushed violently. She wanted to show him the
door; only her conventional respect for his age and his
calling restrained her. "I've took keer o' my young'uns so fer
without no help from no preacher," she retorted.

"Have you?" Brother Pointer rose and looked down at her
sternly. "Have you loved them childern, Berthy, like they
was yourn? You know you ain't; nary one of 'em only
Clance. They'll come a time when you can't help them
childern no more. Then you'll wisht you'd a-helped 'em
while you had a chanst." His expression softened. "Berthy,
listen here, pore girl, I don't aim to be hard on you—"

"You needn't to pore girl me!" Bertha cried, stung to the
heart. "Ain't I got enough to put up with as it is? You tend to
your business and I'll tend to mine!"

He turned away and picked up his ragged wool cap. "I ben
a-tendin' to mine the best way I knowed how," he said
humbly. "I'll hate it right bad if'n it makes you feel hard to

me, Berthy. But you won't be the first one; no, ner you won't be the last.''

Such sadness and resignation were in the old man's tone that Bertha, even in her churned-up condition of mind, could not be unmoved. "I ain't got no hard feelin's," she said dully.

He brightened. "That makes me feel right good. I thank you kindly. Now don't you think I didn't hate to hurt you! I hated it right bad, I tell you I did. Don't you want I should say a prayer right here fer us both? I need it worse'n you. We're both of us sinners. Le's us go ast Him to show us what to do.''

But this was too much. Bertha shook her head, without speaking.

"All right, then," the old man said at last, with sorrow; and, putting on his cap, he turned toward the door. On the threshold he looked back. "If'n ever you need me—"

Bertha nodded, not rising. He closed the door behind him.

Prayers indeed! Bertha's chest ached with the pain, confusion and self-accusation she could not express. An outburst of passionate crying would have relieved her, but she could not cry. "He knows a lot about how things is with me, now don't he?—and him a preacher and a man!" she fumed. But she knew herself surprised that he did know so much, and humiliated too. It was not that she feared he would tattle to anyone else. She knew he would not. "Likely he'll keep a-pesterin' me all the time, though, like he does Doc," she thought. "I ain't a-goin' to put up with it if he does. It ain't none o' his never-minds what I think or how I act. Ner it ain't none o' God's neither that I c'n see. God never done nothin' to keep me outen trouble. Seems like He's jest hell-bent to make trouble fer me.''

She had quailed, as seldom before in all her life, when he told her she wanted more than Jeff Plant's affection. It was one thing to know it within, and another to have it dragged out into the light of day.

And there was more to it than that, too, she told herself, chafing. Maybe she did want more, but if she had that—"I ain't sech a fool as I look!'' she shouted mentally after the departed preacher. "I reckon I know what I want jest about as well as you do! Maybe I would like to have him stuck on me. But I don't have to have him, you hear me? I don't have to have him! I c'd git along all right with jest the other. This way I ain't got nothin', nary a thing! I ain't even got nothin' to help me out with Clance.''

The imagined tirade ended here, abruptly, and Bertha knew that she could no longer escape being confronted with the real anguish Brother Pointer's rebuke had put upon her. He had lined her other children up in a row and made her look at them, and accused her of not loving them and caring for them; and from this sterner indictment there was no escape, though she tried desperately to find one. "Don't it make no differ'nce that Clance is worth the whole kit and bilin' of 'em put together?'' she demanded. "I take keer of all of 'em jest the same. I don't never favor one of 'em over the rest.''

But she knew that this was only superficially true. Her strong sense of justice had nothing to do with love, and her want of love for them was the root of the matter, as the clear-sighted old preacher had seen and plainly said. "They'll come a time when you can't help them children no more. You'll wisht then you'd a-helped 'em while you had a chanst.'' Only Bertha herself, and God if He ever listened, knew how often she had heard this warning before.

She wiped her hot face with her apron and went to the window. The sky was purplish grey and ominous. There was no wind. In the distance, beyond the Bend, she could see smoke rising from the stovepipe chimney of the vacant shack Brother Pointer sometimes used when he stayed in Weary Water over night. He was there now, she supposed, and praying for her to that God of his. He would be down on his rheumatic knees, the "terrible crystal" showering its colors about him.

Bertha cast a scathing glance upward at the insensible clouds. "You c'n stay right in there with Brother Pointer fer all I keer,'' she muttered. "I ain't got no more use fer You than You got fer me!'' She heard Ardeth fretting in the bedroom and, turning her broad back on Omnipotence, went to the child.

XI

It was nearly two weeks before she saw Jeff again. He came to the farm one Friday after school to see her. He found her in the back yard, chopping firewood. The swirling feathers of the year's first snow blew hither and thither in the wind. Ardeth, capped and mittened and swathed to the eyes in a pink woolen scarf, staggered about picking up chunks of wood and dropping them again.

Bertha wore no wrap except her shabby grey sweater. She was bareheaded, as usual, and her hands were red with the cold, but she would not bother with putting on Tim's work gloves. As Jeff came up to the gate she rested her axe on a chunk and greeted him shyly. "Howdy, Mr. Plant," she said, her eyes glowing with irrepressible joy.

"Good Lord, Bertha," Jeff remonstrated mildly, entering and seating himself on the top rail of the fence, "haven't you got enough menfolks around here to do this sort of thing for you?"

Bertha laughed breathlessly. "I like to do it. It rests me. The men gits all the good jobs all the time, seems like." She hesitated. "Didn't you—wouldn't you like to go in the house, Mr. Plant, and set down comfortable?"

"This suits me," Jeff replied, "if you're warm enough."

"I ain't never cold," Bertha assured him. "Seems like I got a reg'lar stove a-burnin' inside of me, winter and summer. 'Tis right chilly out today, though."

"Yes, more snow before night, I expect." Jeff squinted at the lowering sky, then glanced across the fields toward the woods, where a tangle of naked boughs and brambles, blue-black in the snow-lighted atmosphere, announced the ragged margins of the river. "Bertha," he began, and paused. "I may as well tell you and get it over with—what I've come for. My conscience is giving me hell. I've been handing out subversive advice to your offspring."

Bertha knitted her brows. "Clance, you mean?"

"Yes."

She drew in her breath. "What's he ben up to now?"

"Nothing. I'm the one that's been up to things. I don't know what you're going to say to me, Bertha, but I told Clance he'd better go away."

She looked at him, puzzled. "Better go away?"

"Yes. Somewhere he can go on with school and his music."

"Run off, you mean?"

"Yes."

Bertha said nothing.

"He could work his way through high school, you know. Lots of boys do. And I thought if he once got away he might find somebody who'd be interested in his talent and give him a lift with his music."

Bertha fingered the axe-handle. "What'd he say?"

Jeff shook his head. "He wouldn't hear of it. I didn't get to first base." He was silent for a moment. "I suppose, after all, it's a good thing I didn't. He's pretty young."

Bertha dissented. "No. You was right. I never thought nothin' about it myself, but you was right." Her hand moved nervously along the handle of the axe. "I wisht Clance would run off!" she burst out passionately. "I wisht to God he would! But he won't. Tim would cut the blood outen him if he catched him and he knows it." She turned slightly aside, trembling. "Anyhow, I don't reckon the little fool'd think he could go off and leave his mammy."

"That's what he said."

An electric joy sprang into Bertha's eyes; she turned farther away to hide it. "He ain't got no sense," she said thickly. "All young 'uns is fools. What good does he think he's a-goin' to do me with Tim?" Suddenly she turned toward Jeff, her face ashen. "Mr. Plant, don't you say nothin' about this here to nobody, but Clance he skeers me sometimes, he's gitin' so big and strong. I'm plumb skeered to have him around much longer with things like they are!"

"So am I, Bertha," Jeff told her honestly.

"What am I a-goin' to do if'n he—" Bertha swallowed. "I wouldn't put it apast him to kill his daddy if'n he got mad enough," she finally brought out, scarcely above a whisper.

Jeff hesitated. "I'll be honest with you, Bertha; that's what scared me. He promised me he would, as sure as shooting. He said 'I'm a-goin' to kill him the first good chanst I git, and I ain't a-leavin' here till I git to do it.'" Jeff laughed, trying to make light of this boyish bravado, but he did not succeed. Both he and Bertha knew that Clarence was not much given to boyish bravado. There was an intense and growing power in the boy. His sullenness was not the sullenness of the defeated, but the sinister brooding of the avenger biding his time.

Jeff, frowning, tried to put his anxiety into words that Bertha would understand. "You see, Bertha, Clance is so full of life he can hardly stand it. It's got to come out of him one way or another. It ought to come out in his music—" Bertha's eyes fell—"and if it doesn't, God only knows what might happen. I wish you could have seen his face the other night when I got him to listen a minute about his fiddling. I swear to you, Bertha, you wouldn't have known it was Clance. It was only a minute, though—he saw I had noticed, and he shut off the lights before you could say Jack Robinson. I couldn't help wondering if anybody'd ever see him looking like that again."

Bertha trembled. The naked appeal in her eyes was too

much for Jeff. He slid off the fence and came to her, taking one of her icy hands in his. He felt it quiver, but she drew it away. "It ain't no use," she said dully. "What's to be will be, I reckon."

"There isn't any way you could talk some sense into Tim?"

She laughed harshly. "Talk sense into Tim! You jest try it yourself oncet, Mr. Plant. Tim he ain't got no brains and he ain't got no heart ner no feelin's, ner he don't keer what he does to nobody else!" She suddenly flushed and lifted her head with dignity. "I'm right mortified, Mr. Plant, sayin' somethin' like that there. I ain't never said nothin' about Tim to other folks before—"

"Don't be a fool, Bertha. I've got eyes in my head. You don't have to tell me how things are. You haven't told me anything I didn't know, or anything the whole place doesn't know, for that matter."

Bertha's face was crimson to the roots of her hair. "No differ'nce what the whole place knows, it ain't my business to be a-runnin' Tim down. He's my man. I married him my own self. Nobody made me."

"Yes—when you were hardly old enough to crawl out of your cradle!"

"That don't make no differ'nce, Mr. Plant. It ain't nobody else's say-so one way or t'other."

"Sorry." Jeff's tone was curt, but his eyes softened again before her misery. "I wouldn't have tried to make it my say-so, Bertha, if it hadn't been for Clance, you know."

She nodded. "You ben mighty good to Clance, Mr. Plant. He thinks a whole lot of you too, I can tell he does." She fumbled vaguely at the axe-handle. "I never aimed to sound so ornery a while ago. Don't you have no hard feelin's to me, Mr. Plant."

"Bertha! Don't you know you're—" Jeff checked himself. "There couldn't be any hard feelings between you and me, Bertha. You know that. Don't worry." As she did not answer, he went on. "Try not to worry too much about Clance, either. It may all work out somehow. He's got good stuff in him. He's your boy too, you know."

Bertha gave him a dumbly grateful look, then dropped her eyes. A whiff of wind attacked her loosened hair, blowing it wildly back from her troubled face.

"I suppose the reason I went overboard," Jeff continued, "was that I wanted to do something for Clance while I can. I won't be here next year, I suppose you know."

Bertha started violently. "You—you ain't a-comin' back?"

He did not notice her face. His eyes at the moment were on the line of woods in the distance. "No."

Bertha remembered what Clarence had told her. "They ain't nobody got mad at you, Mr. Plant? Mr. Baker never—"

He smiled. "No, they're not firing me, Bertha. But my book's done now and on its way to the publishers, and I have to get a job pretty soon that pays a little more than this one does. My girl's getting back from Paris before long, and this time I don't think I'll let her off—not if my book gets published, anyway." He looked at Bertha now and was startled by her pallor, though by this time she had her features under control. "Why, Bertha! Don't look so tragic about it; I'm not going off tomorrow. Claire won't even be back in this country before Christmas, and I'm finishing out the school term anyway. By next spring we'll think of something to do about Clance, you and I between us. Don't worry."

Bertha stared at the ground, The agony in her eyes, although he misinterpreted it, disturbed him, and he tried to laugh reassuringly. "I don't believe I ever did tell you about Claire, did I? Well, you see she wants to be an artist, and she won this scholarship to study in Paris, so I thought I'd put in the time trying to write a book, so—"

Bertha interrupted him. "What was that there you said—a artist?"

"Well, in Claire's case, a painter. She paints pictures."

"Pictures?" Bertha was still dazed. "I never heared of no woman done that fer a livin'."

"Sometimes I wish I hadn't either," Jeff said, a little wryly. "No, I don't mean a word of that, Bertha. Claire's wonderful. If painting's her job, she's got a right to do it, woman or no woman. When men stop trying to nail women's feet to the kitchen floor, we may get a surprise or two, at least I think so. I've thought so for a long time—especially since I came to Weary Water." He smiled. "Take you, now, Bertha. Why, a woman like you, if she'd ever got a chance, could have done anything. With that quick mind of yours, and that big strong splendid body—"

Bertha started; was he insulting her? But no, he was looking straight at her, not ashamed at all. It must be he still did not know what "body" meant here. Her white face had gone crimson, and she turned it away for a moment. He was still talking, but she did not hear what he said. She suddenly felt like screaming at him to go. She could not bear his presence any longer. Talk, talk, talk, and all the time her insides turning over. Was she going to be sick again?

He had stopped talking now and stepped down from the fence. "Well, I must be on my way. Good-bye, Bertha. Don't worry."

XII

Brother Pointer did not, as Bertha had bitterly prophesied, "keep a-pesterin' her" all the time. He only watched her. She knew that he watched her, and she resented it fiercely. In a way she resented, too, his failure to admonish her, just as she always resented it when she prepared for a battle with Tim and no battle arose, and just as she had resented it when Mr. Plant remained oblivious of what she had so feared he would discover. None of it made any sense, and Bertha had given up trying to put sense into it. Either she was a born fool or all women were fools and she was the star example. She suspected the latter.

Brother Pointer's single admonition, however, had not been without its effects. By main force she had restrained herself from making any active effort to see the teacher. And what had she accomplished by it, when the mere sight of him sitting there on the fence was enough to fill her with torment for weeks to come? The memory of his visit was alternate brandy and brine. The tone in which he had said "There couldn't be any hard feelings between you and me, Bertha," and the clasp of his hand, from which she had so conscientiously and needlessly withdrawn her own, came back to her again and again, overwhelming as a warm bright wave. The understanding with which he had met her fears for Clarence and the honesty with which he had shared them made a shelter of love and relief for her terrified heart. But those scorching other words—"Lovely thing, isn't she?" "My girl"; "Claire's wonderful"—were like deposits of salt in an open wound. Fancy talk, town talk, talk only suited to women like that there one in the picture, that looked like she didn't have no insides at all! "I'd jest like to know whereabouts she'd put 'em if she did have," Bertha fumed at the kitchen mirror with a fine show of scorn.

The mirror gave back its usual hateful reply, reflecting her broad shoulders, deep bosom and smouldering eyes. "You'd think a man'd want a woman that looked like a woman," she fretted. "Anyhow, Bud Wilkerson said my hair was pretty. I bet he wouldn't look twicet at a woman like that." But there was little encouragement in this, for she did not believe it. Bud was no specialist in pulchritude, he liked it all. And the woman in the picture, Bertha bitterly conceded, was "right pretty."

At the heart-stopping news that Jeff was going away she had cast to the winds her recent and prudent resolves. He wanted nothing of her and he never would, but while he was here she might as well enjoy it. It couldn't hurt him or her or anybody else if she let herself think of him, dream of him, talk with him, borrow his books. And what more could she do, with him as good as married? The fact that she herself was married had ceased to inhibit her. The way Jeff had spoken of his "girl", even while she felt herself stabbed by it, had given her a new conception of marriage and what it might become. With her usual forthrightness and perspicuity, she arrived almost at once at the conclusion that marriage with Tim Mallory was no marriage. She ceased, therefore, to suffer his shame for him; she had more than enough of her own to cope with now. If he wanted to make a sickening show of himself, that was his business, not hers. She neither owed nor would give him the tribute of sharing it.

Further, she had begun to see that she must make this plain to Clarence. The boy ought to know by this time which side she was on, but perhaps he did not. Perhaps he still linked her with Tim in spite of all, still thought of them both as pulling against him and the other children. Both she and Clarence had witnessed the flogging of Clovis, she from the kitchen window, he from the barn. She had seen him standing there gripping the handle of a milk pail, and now she thought she remembered his looking at her. He had not expected her to interfere, for he knew as well as she did that it was useless. But he must have expected something. What else could it be? What else could it be but to have her make known to him, clearly and without equivocation, that she had no part in all this and never would have?

She knew she must try, and she did not know how to begin. She waited and watched for an opportunity and found it one evening at supper in early December, when Tim for once was silent and the children emboldened to chatter. They were excited; Mr. Plant, Daisy announced, had told them that day that he was going to get up "a entertainment" at the school for Christmas.

"What kind?" Bertha asked, instantly alert at the mention of Jeff's name. "Speak pieces, you mean?"

Daisy bounced in her chair. "The littlest kids is a-goin' to have pieces to speak. Us big ones, we git to be in the tabblows."

"Tabblows? What's them?"

Daisy found her powers of explanation overchallenged and looked at Opal, whose pretty, empty face was also alight. "Them's kind o' pictures, Maw, with real people in 'em. One of 'em's the Virgil Mary and the manger and shepherds."

"Opal she wants to be the Virgil Mary," Woodrow put in slyly.

"Shet up," said Opal, flushing. She turned to her mother. "They light red lights on 'em, Maw. It's awful pretty, Mr. Plant says it is. He's goin' to town next week to buy the things. Mr. Plant wants Clance should play a tune on his fiddle—"

"Mr. Plant kin keep right on a-wantin'," Clarence interrupted, scowling.

"Well, anyhow," continued Opal, tossing her frizzled head, "he's aimin' to have a Christmas tree and a Santy Claus. Bud Wilkerson, he's a-goin' to be the Santy Claus."

"An' b-b-b-bring p-p-p-presents!" stammered Clovis irrepressibly, with a half fearful side glance at his father.

"I hope I git a dorine," said Opal dreamily. At Bertha's obvious puzzlement she explained. "It's a little box like, on a chain, with powder in it—"

Bertha was instantly alert. "Where at did you see one o' them? Who's got one? Who showed you one?

Opal shrank, and Bertha, remembering Tim's presence, forebore to press the question at the moment. She was aware that Tim was swelling and girding; he had been ignored long enough, it was time to assert himself. "Derned foolishness," he now commented, taking a noisy drink of water.

The children held their breath, and so also did Bertha. If he forbade them any part in the entertainment, it would be like the end of the world for them all; even Opal was an eager child in the face of this glowing prospect. And, wonder of wonders, it had stopped their quarreling. Opal's command to Woodrow to "shet up" had been absent-minded, not ill-natured. Moreover, Bertha's heart was churning and pounding; Mr. Plant would need help, plenty of it, for a project like that! "If you're a-goin' to be in the tabblows, Opal," she said with unaccustomed gentleness, "you better start soakin' your hands in buttermilk. I read somewheres that'd make a person's hands right soft."

Opal, stunned at this unexpected suggestion from her mother, said nothing. Clarence's lip curled. "She better soak her dern fool head in it instid of her hands."

Tim turned on him furiously. "Who ast you to put in your two cents' worth? Shet up, you hear me?"

All life was suspended for a moment. Bertha, though she did not know it, was praying. But Clarence's remark had fallen like a tossed coin, deciding the issue of the entertainment once for all. If Tim had intended to quash the children's hopes, nothing on earth would induce him to do so now. He said no more, but shoved back his chair, wiped his mouth as usual on his sleeve, and left the table. The children beamed. Bertha's own face lit with relief, and she caught Clarence's eye. She saw, incredulously, that he was suppressing a grin. God love him, God love him for smartness, he'd done it a-purpose! She wanted to rush upon him and cover his face and hands with maudlin kisses. Perhaps Clarence knew it, for he made his escape.

The other children broke into a Babel of talk, explaining, describing, laughing, interrupting each other; it was a spectacle. Bertha's heart smote her. "This here's the way it ort to be all the time. Pore young 'uns, they're jest like their mammy—they ain't got nothin' *to* do but fight and fuss."

She thought of Molly Pointer. Had Molly more? But yes, Brother Pointer probably "made over" Molly. He told her stories, likely. He took her walking with him and showed her things. He made himself little like her and played with her. Why hadn't she, Bertha, realized this before? "It ain't so all-fired easy, though, when they's six," she defended herself. "And Molly ain't got no daddy like Tim to skeer her."

Still, she saw at last that something might be done, and hope and resolution rose within her. She looked across at Opal's radiant face and suddenly felt a passionate sympathy; if Opal wanted to be "the Virgil Mary", Bertha hoped with all her heart that Mr. Plant would let her. "Likely he will," she thought, "she's any amount the prettiest, and one of the oldest."

Somehow she got them all blissfully to bed, and sat down alone—Tim had made off for an evening at Boney Bartlett's—to contemplate and marvel at her own unheralded bliss. "Gittin' myself all worked up over a play-party!" she scoffed. "Them tabblows, though, I reckon they'll be right pretty."

She tried to remember pictures she had seen, to plan how she ought to dress Opal for her part. "Mr. Plant'll tell me, I reckon," she thought happily, rocking.

The kitchen door opened and Clarence came in, alone. He

hesitated when he saw her sitting there, but after a moment came and sat down himself, not taking off his cap and windbreaker. "I ain't sleepy," he explained grudgingly, as though she had asked him.

"I ain't neither, Clance. Le's us jest set here a little while and talk."

He looked at her suspiciously. "Talk about what?"

"Oh, nothin'. Jest talk." Bertha paused. "This here entertainment—don't you like it, Clance?"

He shrugged. "It's all right fer the kids. 'Tain't none o' my business."

"You shore made it your business tonight," said Bertha proudly.

Clarence's eyelids flickered. "Aw, he gives me a pain!"

Bertha nodded. "He gives me a pain too, Clance," she answered calmly. Clarence, startled, looked up at her, and she laughed. "Why land o' livin', Clance, you must 'a' knowed it. You must 'a' knowed I felt like throwin' things at him"

Again she saw him struggle not to smile. "I thought fer a minute there he'd tear me apart."

"So'd I," agreed Bertha, shivering. "You done good."

She could hardly believe it when he did not repulse her. For a moment, as he arose, her heart stood still; but he was only taking off his jacket, and when he had done so he sat down again. He was here, she was actually "having a talk" with him! Always before he had been straining for flight; his hand on the doorknob, his glance flung over his shoulder. Here he was sitting with her face to face, letting her talk to him and talking to her! Bertha's heart sang. "I 'uz right sorry you didn't feel like you could play," she ventured mildly.

He made a disgusted sound.

"I was jest a-thinkin'," Bertha continued, measuring every word, "when Opal was a-tellin' about them there tabblows, it'd be mighty pretty if'n some music was playin' behind 'em."

"Let Mr. Plant play on the organ, then."

Bertha sighed. "Well, yes, I reckon he could. I reckon he'll have to." Suddenly she leaned forward. "Clance, why'n't you play me a little tune right now? I ain't heered you play nothin' sence Hec was a pup."

He stared at her. "You want to wake up all them kids?"

"It won't wake 'em up. Don't make no differ'nce if'n it does," Bertha's eyes were shining. "You play me a dance tune, like you played at Milltown."

Clarence grinned openly this time. "You want to dance?"

Bertha laughed. "Clance, I b'lieve to my soul I do!" She ran to the fiddle and took it down from the wall, thrusting it forcibly into his hands. "You might think I don't know how, but I ain't fergot." She cake-walked across the room to inaudible music, with a rhythm and recklessness that were irresistible. Clarence lifted his bow and began to play *Turkey in the Straw*. Bertha laughed aloud as she danced the familiar measures, and when he deliberately speeded the tempo she matched him in speed and abandon, her magnificent hair coming loose from its pins and falling over her shoulders. Opal and Daisy, blinking and open-mouthed, stood barefooted in the doorway, but neither she nor Clarence saw them. As Bertha turned in their direction, they fled.

She sank, laughing and breathless, back into her chair. "That was fine, Clance." She began to gather up her fallen hair for pinning.

"Why'n't you jest leave it like that there? It looks all right," said Clarence, and was instantly panic-stricken. "I got to go to bed," he added as her mouth opened. "I'm sleepy."

There was no sleep at all for Bertha that magic night. Tim, coming in half an hour later and finding her sitting in a daze, with her hair still down and her hands lying idle on the chair-arms, treated her to some five minutes of his best brand of sarcasm, inquiring with elaborate leers and gestures whether she had decided to beat Opal's time and be the Virgil Mary herself in the teacher's tabblows. "You look plumb holy," he assured her, grinning. "Maybe I better go git Mr. Plant and have him come see."

Bertha gave him a lofty look and pinned up her hair. She

was far beyond Tim's power to disturb her. If she looked "plumb holy", it was little more than she felt. Not often in her cramped and dismal life had she known active happiness of any kind, and this evening, with its rapid succession of joys, was like the "showers of blessing" Brother Pointer so often mentioned in his sermons. The young 'uns were happy; she had found something, maybe, she could do for them; Mr. Plant would certainly need help with the Christmas entertainment; and, on top of all this, miracle of miracles, Clarence had smiled at her, talked to her, fiddled for her dancing. And he had said her hair looked all right hanging down!

She had even forgotten, for the moment, that Mr. Plant was going away. She had forgotten the woman in the picture.

Tim was puzzled at his failure to annoy her. He glowered at her across the bedroom as she entered. "You c'n git one thing through your head right now, my lady," he admonished her. "I ain't a-puttin' out one red cent on them there Christmas doin's. You needn't to come a-whinin' to me fer money. If'n them young 'uns can't be in it like they are, they'll stay outen it fer good and all. You hear me?"

Even this did not alarm Bertha or perturb her. She would manage. She would get what was needed, though she had to steal it. "I'm a-headin' fer hell anyhow, whichever way I take a notion to go. What differ'nce does it make?" she ruminated with entire placidity.

She thought of hell again and many times that night, long after Tim was asleep and oblivious, and found herself drunken with its evil beauty. Brother Pointer's shimmering heaven was nothing to it. Since she had to go, she might as well go dancing, with Clance playing *Turkey in the Straw* not far behind her. They were two of a kind, she and Clance, and maybe they belonged there. This world obviously had very little use for either of them, and what could God possibly do with them in heaven?

She did not want God's love or Brother Pointer's. She wanted Jeff Plant's, and only in hell, it seemed, could she hope to get it. Or on the road there, the spangled road to Christmas, where at every turn she would meet Jeff Plant and adore him. Though she stood with him in a very pit of flame, with the fire creeping nearer and nearer every moment, it would be bliss and nothing but bliss to the end.

Morning found her, for all her wakeful night, unwearied and still burgeoning with plans. When Opal approached her hesitantly just before leaving for school she gave scant attention, though she saw that the girl looked rather uneasy.

"Maw," Opal began, and then stopped, looking down.

"What's the matter?" said Bertha absently. "Cat got your tongue?"

Opal looked up, then away. "Maw, it—it was Mamie Johnson had that there dorine—"

Bertha stared. She had completely forgotten the matter. "You mean to tell me you ben hangin' around—"

"No, I ain't," said Opal hurriedly. "I—"

"Well, you mind you don't, young lady, do you hear me? I meant ever' word I said to you before. You jest let me hear o' you a-hangin' around Mamie Johnson or that boy either, and I'll plumb take you apart, you mark my words."

"I jest seen her with it in the store," muttered Opal. "Maw—"

But Bertha was already back in her darling dream. "You better git on to school before books is took up. It's near about time fer the last bell to ring right now. Where's Clance at? If'n he's already went to school, he didn't eat no breakfast."

Opal looked at her with an inscrutable face. "I don't know where Clance is at and I don't keer!" She snatched up her schoolbooks and flounced away, not looking back.

This was unexampled and inexcusable "sass" for which Bertha would ordinarily have hauled Opal back for a reckoning, and in very short order. She scarcely heard it. They were all out of the house now except Ardeth, who was placidly eating a biscuit soaked in ham gravy. Bertha waited until the last crumb had disappeared, wiped the child's face with a damp towel, bundled her in wraps and sent her outside to play. Returning, she piled and washed the breakfast dishes swiftly and was about to go on to her other housework as usual, when an unfamiliar lassitude overtook her. "I c'n make up them there beds in ten minutes whenever I feel like it," she thought. "I don't know's they's any law says I got to do 'em right now." And, for the first time in her life, she sat down at mid-morning, in a disordered house, and gave herself over completely to thoughts of her love.

XIV

Weary Water, as a rule, made little of Christmas. The Christmas tree was a legend brought from town and nothing more. Children did not hang up their stockings. Some of the farmers brought home "Christmas tricks" at approximately the holiday season—a few oranges, a little cheap candy, a gaudy toy or two—and distributed them casually, not saving them for any particular day. Even at church there was small mention of the holiday's significance, and no thought was taken of special rites or celebrations. This year's plan aroused consternation as well as interest; it looked expensive and was therefore alarming. Baker was the only one of the farmers who approached the prosperous. Probably Tim Mallory was next in line, for Tim was parsimonious to a degree. He did not earn much, but what he earned he hoarded. Bud Wilkerson had not much cash on hand at any time, and to provide fancy costumes for his children would require some skimping and scheming, but Bud did not mind. He was pleased that the children, not only his but all the others, should rejoice; he was more than pleased to be cast as Santa Claus; he liked Jeff Plant and was always ready to help him. The others were doubtful, though not ill-disposed toward the project. "Likely they won't be no more revivals yit awhile," was the consensus. Sister Cory Plummer, it was rumored, had "had a call" to go down to Arkansas, and Brother Pointer was preaching somewhere else. He had not been seen in Weary Water for two weeks.

When it became known that Mr. Plant had foreseen the financial difficulties and intended to bear the total expense himself—tree, costumes, lights, decorations, and presents— there was a sensation. "Don't look like he'd have that much money to spare," Mrs. Bartlett said to Bertha in the store. "Maybe he's a-workin' it in cahoots with Doc Brumbaugh. They do say Doc's got a-plenty salted away."

Bertha's one anxiety rolled with a thump from her shoulders. If Mr. Plant was paying for the costumes, there was nothing at all for her to worry about. Clovis and Woodrow, they had told her in excited stammers, were to be shepherds in the Nativity scene. Daisy was to be the mother of a family of children gathered about the tree on Christmas Eve.

Mrs. Bartlett, in her interest, was almost vivacious. "They say he's brung more truck out from town!" she cried. "Bud Wilkerson says he's got presents for everybody—not jest the kids, but ever'body in the place! And he brung Bud a Santy Claus suit, with whiskers and all. And a big sack to put the things in, and lights. And some funny kind o' powder to burn red and yeller and green, and a lot o' little shiny balls, all colors, and little shiny horns full o' candy and nuts. He wants the young 'uns to string popcorn and cranb'ries. I got to keep a eye on my kids, I c'n tell you. If'n I didn't watch what they're doin' every minute, they wouldn't be a cranb'ry left in the store."

Bertha made perfunctory reply and took her leave, her excitement rising to new heights. All the way home she fought an internal battle with her impulse to go to the school and see the things. She had to see Mr. Plant about the costumes. But he knew that just as well as she did, so he'd probably send for her or come to see her. But he was certainly, Bertha thought, taking his time! Several days had gone by already, and no word from him; no news of the party except what the children brought home. They, of course, knew no other topic now. Clarence remained aloof but was indulgent. His thrust at Opal had been his only comment, and he had even tied a knot in a thread for Daisy, who, during Tim's frequent absences from the house, was stealthily popping corn and stringing it.

Bertha felt it almost impossible to wait. Why must she, after all? It was surely a legitimate errand, going to school to consult about the costumes. Brother Pointer was away somewhere; he would not see her, and there was nobody else who would think much of it just now. She couldn't very well be thought to be carrying on with Mr. Plant before a roomful of young 'uns. No, she reminded herself grimly, and she couldn't very well *be* carrying on with him in those circumstances, either. "That's the trouble," she thought, and laughed aloud.

She decided to go that afternoon at three-thirty. School would be out at four; she could see him then, maybe, for a moment alone.

She dressed and arranged her hair with unusual attention. The mirror told her she had done very well. Indeed, its comment startled her, for no such face had looked from it ever before. No such bright, expectant eyes, no such glowing cheeks. And certainly it had never smiled at her.

She would have to take Ardeth along, of course, so she decided to ride and took Jess out of the stall. The winter air, crisp and crackling, filled her lungs with freshness and her heart with ecstasy. She was hardly mounted, with the child before her, when she began to gallop, and the short ride was over before it had well begun. She dismounted, lifted Ardeth down and tied Jess to the school yard fence, but she stood hesitating there for several minutes, abashed by her own unaccustomed daring and enterprise. Now that she was here, she knew she should not have come. But she had come, and that was all there was to it.

She took Ardeth's hand, therefore, made her way to the building and knocked on the door. She could hear Jeff's voice and his footsteps approaching, and her pulses pounded. He opened the door. "Why, Berth—Mrs. Mallory!" he exclaimed, offering his hand. "You know, I've always wished you'd come to see us. Come in—come in!" He helped her off with her coat, helped her unwind the woolen scarf from her head. "Here, take my chair—I'm standing up anyway. Put Ardeth's things over here. That's right. Comfortable?" He indicated some figures on the blackboard. "We're just about to wind up an arithmetic lesson." He spoke to his pupils. "Best behavior now; we've got company." He turned to Bertha. "This will only take a few minutes, Mrs. Mallory."

"You go right ahead, Mr. Plant," Bertha managed to say. She was acutely aware of the children's curious glances and of the assiduity with which her own children avoided her eyes. Visitors to Weary Water school were infrequent indeed, and the Mallory children did not know whether to feel honored or disgraced. Until they found out, they did not dare look up. Bertha had caught one glimpse of Clarence's astonished eyes, but now, like the others, he looked away from her as Mr. Plant took up his pointer and explained the problem on the board.

Bertha did not hear a word of what Jeff was saying. She heard only his voice, so dear to her and so different from any other. Beyond him, piled in a corner of the room, were the "things" that had excited the community. She saw half-open packages of dry-goods, lengths of fabric in many different colors, and other boxes and bags that shot forth gleams of particolored light. An old reading chart was draped with strung cranberries and popcorn. On the wall above the chart he had pinned several pictures; one, the largest, of the Madonna bending over the manger, with sheep and cows and shepherds and the Wise Men gathered about. The others were gaily assorted holiday scenes. On top of the organ lay Bud's Santa Claus suit.

"That will be all for today," she heard Jeff saying. He took out his watch. "One." The children put their books away. "Two." They rose and stood beside their desks. "Three.

Keep a straight line, now." They marched decorously out of the room, bursting into clamor the moment they reached the cloakroom, and Jeff turned to Bertha, smiling and raising his voice above the din of voices and clattering lunch-pails. "Here, Bertha, let me take Ardeth off your hands. She can sit at a desk like a big girl now, and draw pictures." He carried the willing Ardeth off the platform and established her at a desk with a slate and pencil. "There. Now we can talk," he exclaimed, turning eagerly back. "Bertha! I'm so glad you came! I've got something to tell you!"

Bertha's lips parted. She had never seen him like this. He was more excited than any of the children. She could not answer him, but he did not wait. He set both hands on her shoulders, gripping them hard, almost shaking them. "Bertha—guess what! I've sold my book. They're going to publish it. I'm a novelist, Bertha!" His eyes were so bright she suspected tears, but he laughed. "You want I should send you a copy when it gits in print?" he asked her, in droll imitation of Weary Water.

"That there'd be right down nice in you, Mr. Plant," said Bertha. She spoke but faintly, for he was very near.

He laughed with delight and suddenly kissed her, twice; first on one flaming cheek and then on the other. "Bertha, you're priceless. I couldn't do without you." He gave her shoulders another hard squeeze and released her. "They sent me a check, you know, an advance on royalties. That's why I'm playing Lord Bountiful all of a sudden." He indicated the pile of merchandise in the corner. "I wanted to do it last year, but I couldn't afford it, and I knew it would be a strain any other way. This time we're going to do it up brown. You and I, Bertha. You'll help me with it, won't you? Look, here's the stuff I got for Opal's mantle."

He pulled a package from the general pile, detached the Nativity picture from the wall, and brought both to her, laying them in her lap. "See, that's how it drapes, the blue stuff, over her head. You can make that for her all right, can't you, Bertha?"

Bertha fingered the soft blue material distractedly. "I

reckon," she managed to say, and, a moment later, "Don't look like it was nothin' more'n a tablecloth."

"That's right. It isn't. It's all in the draping, you see." He went back to the pile and returned with a bundle of something brown. "This is what I got for the shepherds—just tow sacks. About all you have to do is cut out necks and armholes, and belt 'em in with rope—I've got the rope too. Oh, yes, I knew there was something. It's about Clovis. Did you know that Clovis has a very good voice?"

Bertha blinked. She could not cope with his rapid talk; how did he expect her to, when he had kissed her? "Voice?"

"He sings like a mocking-bird. I'll bet you never even knew it." Jeff rummaged about the organ and brought back a sheet of music. "This is *Gesu Bambino*, one of the loveliest Christmas songs I know. I want Clovis to sing it for us that evening. I tried to get Clance to learn it on the fiddle—no use, of course. But Clovis can sing it anyway, all by himself. Like to hear it? Here's the way it goes." He went back to the organ, twirled the stool, and sat down. Bertha, listening, heard the music but vaguely. " 'Tis pretty," she said indistinctly when he had finished. "Clovis is right timid, though, fer singin' before folks," she added doubtfully.

"I know it. That's why I told you. I want you to work on him. Let him sing it for you at home; he'll get used to it. Whew!" Jeff laughed and sat down on Ardeth's desk. "I've talked myself out of breath. But it's pretty exciting, you know, about the book."

Bertha was silent. Her body was thrumming with joy, but her mind was disturbed. There was a thorn in it somewhere, she knew, for her. Jeff must have felt her uneasiness over his excitement, for he rose again and came to her, taking her hand. "Bertha, I want to tell you—"

There was a discreet knock at the half-open door. Brother Pointer stood there, amiable but troubled. "Howdy, Mr. Plant. Howdy, Mis' Mallory; how's all yore folks at home?"

Bertha made shift to murmur "All right," but she was discomposed. He must have seen Jeff bend toward her and take her hand.

The old man entered and took off his woollen cap. "I jest got back, Mr. Plant, from over in Foster," he said. "I heard you was fixin' to have a Christmas frolic."

"That's right, Brother Pointer. We're planning quite a shindig. Songs and recitations and tableaux, and a Santa Claus and a tree."

Brother Pointer smiled. "The childern's right tickled about it all, I reckon." He hesitated. "I ain't jest sure, Mr. Plant, what that there is—them tabblows?"

Jeff explained. Brother Pointer looked a little doubtful. "It ain't like play-actin', is it, Mr. Plant?"

"Not exactly, and not much. Just pictures, Brother Pointer, most of them religious. There won't be anything you'd disapprove of, I'm sure." He explained the Nativity scene, and the old preacher nodded. "I reckon it's all right to do, Mr. Plant. If'n you'd like to have me say a word or two to the folks whilst they're all together that night, I'd be mighty glad to oblige."

Bertha boiled with irritation, and even Jeff hesitated; but he said, "Why, that will be fine, Brother Pointer. I'll appreciate it."

The old man nodded. "Glad to help you out. Well, I must be gittin' on; it's pretty late." He peered out the window at the darkening sky. "I'm a-goin' your way, Mis' Mallory, if so be you want comp'ny."

Bertha was brusque. "I got Jess waitin' outside."

Brother Pointer put on his cap. "Well, I must go." His eyes met Bertha's squarely; she could not avoid them. "I'm afeared it's gittin' right down late a'ready," he repeated.

XV

She was not surprised when Brother Pointer called again next day. She expected him. "Yes, and I'm ready fer him too," she muttered. "He better not try to push me too clost to the wall." She seethed with fury every time she remembered his offer to accompany her home. "He knowed good and well I was ahorseback. He seen Jess a-standin' there before he come in."

She had been, indeed, so confused and exasperated by his interference that it had taken her hours to put him out of her mind, though mind as well as body strained toward the moment when she could forget him—forget him and remember that Jeff had kissed her. Until that moment came, at least she must talk of Jeff. She felt like babbling of him, but that would not do, and she retained enough sense to realize it. But she talked far more than usual that night at supper, several times causing Tim to shoot her a look of suspicion. "What'd Mr. Plant say?" she would ask the children at every new remark concerning the party, her voice as well as her heart caressing the name. And, while they eagerly told her, she sat and smiled. She puzzled even the children, but the change in her was only too welcome to them. They didn't have to understand it to enjoy it. When Tim, becoming restive, commanded them all to "shet up that yammerin' and let a man eat his supper in some kind o' peace," Bertha subsided into silence and happiness. She forgot Brother Pointer for a time, and her blood leaped secretly and high as she felt the touch of Jeff's lips again on her face.

She sought out Clarence in private, later that evening, and made one more effort to get him to play at the party. She spoke to him with a new freedom, even briskly. "Clance, why'nt you learn that there piece—what's he call it? Bam—bam somethin'." She laughed. "I can't call to mind how it goes."

"That there's a dago name." Clarence informed her. "Eye-talian. He says it means Baby Jesus or somethin'."

"He played it fer me there on the organ today. It's right pretty, Clance."

" 'Tain't sech a bad tune. I ain't a-playin' it, though."

His tone was final, and Bertha knew it was useless. "I reckon Mr. Plant'll hate that right bad," she said regretfully. "Seems like it'd be kind o' nice to do it fer him, Clance. Him givin' presents to ever'body and all."

Clarence scowled. "He ain't a-givin' me no presents. I wouldn't take none." Bertha sighed.

"I got to go see about somethin'," Clarence said vaguely. Bertha took what comfort she could from his making an excuse; he would not have done so, she knew, until very lately. There must have been something for him as well as for her in the memory of that short evening together. He had not spoken roughly to her a single time since. He was no more amenable to control than ever, but he seemed to be trying to thank her, in his blind way, for letting him know she was on his side against Tim. He did not love her, maybe, but he respected her now that he knew what she thought.

Bertha gave herself for the rest of the night to her dream. It was not until late next morning that she thought of Brother Pointer. When she did, she consciously gathered her forces together. "He kin be awful tejus when he wants to. I ort to jest tell him right out to leave me alone. If'n he gits too brash I will, too, you mark my words!"

She meant it. She would if she could. It was not his age alone, she knew, that restrained her. It was something indomitable in him that mastered her. In some way, for all her strength, he was the stronger.

She could not, therefore, cast off all uneasiness when she saw him coming, but she steeled herself at least to give him as good as he sent.

He came, as before, while the children were in school and Ardeth in the bedroom taking her nap. "Evenin', Mis' Mallory," he greeted her courteously. "It's still right cold out, ain't it? But you got a nice fire."

Bertha gave him the rocker and sat down on a hard chair. "Jest lay your cap on the table, Brother Pointer," she said civilly. "Don't you want to take your coat off while you're in here?"

"Well, maybe I better," Brother Pointer conceded. Bertha could see that he was uneasy too. His hands trembled a little as he unbuttoned the coat. She took it and laid it aside, and they sat down. There was an awkward silence. Bertha made no attempt to relieve it.

Brother Pointer held out his hands to the stove. "That there feels good," he remarked, and smiled at her. "I 'uz right cold when I come in, but this is fine, Mis' Mallory, it certainly is." He hesitated. "Seems like I ain't ben good and warm sence yistiddy mornin'. I had me a mighty bad skeer about my little Molly."

"She sick again?" asked Bertha perfunctorily.

The old man shook his head. "No, she ain't sick, praise the Lord. But she come pretty near fallin' over the side of a gully." He shivered. "We was out walkin', and they was a rabbit jumped outen a briarpatch and went a-kitin' off, and Molly a-kitin' after him before I c'd ketch her. Ef I hadn't 'a' got there jest in time to grab her by the skirt—" He shook his head. "Childern's awful heedless little things, ain't they, Mis' Mallory?"

Bertha looked him in the eyes. "Childern knows pretty well what they want sometimes, Brother Pointer."

He met her gaze. "They think they do, Berthy."

Bertha tossed her head and did not answer.

"Molly thought she wanted that there rabbit,' he went on slowly. "But if'n I hadn't a-grabbed her skirt in time, what would 'a' happened? She'd 'a' fell over that there clift and ben broke to pieces; I can't a-bear so much as to think of it!" Brother Pointer brushed his eyes with his hand. "That child's my own child's child. I'm plumb wropped up in her, that I am. Sometimes I think I love her more'n I ort to. But I reckon our blessed Lord'll fergive me fer that. He knows we ain't none of us much more'n heedless childern."

"I bet Molly didn't thank you none fer pullin' her back," said Bertha shrewdly.

Brother Pointer's lips twitched. "No, I got to admit you're right there, Berthy. She didn't. She felt right hard to me all the rest o' the day. But what good would it 'a' done her to chase that rabbit, if'n she was a-layin' there crippled or maybe dead? She couldn't 'a' ketched the rabbit anyhow, and my old heart would 'a' broke to pieces fer nothin'. Ain't it awful to think o' waste like that?"

Bertha did not reply. Her feelings were mixed. He had not made up the story. It must have happened. He had neither the imagination nor the deviousness to contrive it. "He's a-workin' it fer all it's worth, jest the same," she thought with a trace of irritated admiration. "He don't leave out a thing he kin squeeze outen it." Aloud she said, after a moment: "Maybe she could 'a' ketched it. How do you know?" As he only looked at her and shook his head, she flamed into anger. "You needn't to try to fool me, Brother Pointer. I know it ain't Molly you're a-worryin' about. It's me. Well, you needn't to. I know what I'm a-doin'. I know what you're a-doin', too. You're a-tryin' to pull me back to that God o' yourn. Well, I don't want no part of Him, you hear me? He ain't done nothin' fer me. What do I keer? He kin fall in a gully Himself fer all o' me—I wouldn't lift nary a finger to pull Him back!"

Brother Pointer's face settled to sternness. "Hesh. Don't you talk thataway to me about my Lord. They ain't no man I'll take it from ner no woman." He controlled himself. "I'm sorry fer you. I'm afeared you're headed fer destruction."

"You think that there's news to me? I 'uz borned that way. That God o' yourn, He wants me to be like that! He taken me and put me under Tim's thumb, and He's ben a-helpin' Tim squeeze the breath outen me ever sence—"

"No, He ain't, Berthy. He ain't. You're right down wrong. He never wants nobody to suffer like you do. You suffer useless. That ain't the way He wants it. People picks out their lives fer theirselves. When they pick 'em out wrong, they suffer, but God ain't to blame. He's always a-waitin' to show 'em what to do. He c'n take them sufferin's and turn 'em into gold. He taken mine, bless His name, and made 'em over, and I got 'em now in my pocket to use fer others. I look like a pore man, Berthy, but I ain't. I'm a rich man, my pockets is never empty. They's nary a pore grievin' soul comes askin' fer help that I ain't got help to give him, blessed be God! I got help fer you too, Berthy, if'n you'd only take it."

"I don't want no help," said Bertha stubbornly. "I know what I'm a-doin'."

The old man sank back in his chair. "I wisht I knowed what to say. You're a fine woman, big and strong and smart—yes, and beautiful too—" Bertha laughed contemptuously, but he was not to be flustered. "Yes, Berthy: even a wore-out old man like me kin see beauty and feel it. They ain't many of us that's beautiful here in this world. It'd do a man good jest to look at it, if it was right. But to see sech beauty lit up with the fires o' hell—"

Bertha laughed again, but this time joyously. "Ain't that funny, Brother Pointer? You pretty near said what I was a-thinkin' myself the other night. I was a-thinkin' the fires o' hell was right pretty."

She hoped to shock him into silence, but she failed. He only nodded. "First time I seen 'em I thought they was pretty too. But I changed my tune when I felt 'em a-lickin' against me. Berthy, humble your heart; thank God fer the blessin's He's give you. God give you that beauty to be a woman with—"

"That's what I figured," said Bertha flippantly. "What elst do you think I'm a-doin', Brother Pointer?"

Brother Pointer sighed. "You're a-bein' a child, Berthy, no bigger ner older'n Molly. You're a-chasin' a rabbit you ain't never goin' to ketch, and you won't let nobody pull you back from the clift. I'm ready; God's ready; you won't have neither one. I'm plumb tuckered out a-thinkin' what to do."

"You better go home and rest, then," Bertha said caustically.

He flinched and got to his feet. "All right, Berthy. I'll go." He put on his coat and cap, trembling. "I feel right sick when a woman acts so hard. It's bad enough in a man. I won't come here to bother you no more, then, Berthy. Good-bye."

Bertha shut the door behind him with a bang, awakening Ardeth. She had borne it once when he told her she would never "ketch her rabbit," but twice was too much. She knew she had hurt him, but she did not care. "He's got it a-comin' to him, the crazy old fool!" she thought bitterly. "Why'n't he leave other people alone and tend to his business? Comin' here tellin' me yarns about Molly and rabbits, like I was a young 'un that had to be humored!—Shet up that cryin' right now, Ardeth, you hear me?"

As for catching her rabbit, she'd show him a thing or two! "I wisht I'd 'a' come right out and told him Mr. Plant kissed me!" she thought. "He knows so much, I'd like to see what he'd say then!"

She was the angrier with him because she knew she had hurt him. His attentions, however presumptuous, were kindly intended. Brother Pointer had no axe to grind. His concern for her soul, if she had one, was genuine; but Bertha had never been sure that she had a soul, and she would have swapped twenty souls, anyway, for one more kiss from Jeff Plant. The substitutes Brother Pointer offered her she neither understood nor wished to understand. They sounded pretty tame to Bertha's rebellious ears. Brother Pointer, to be sure, did not seem to find them so. Every time he spoke of his own relation to his God, his old voice rang like a trumpet.

Standing there in his tattered old clothes, bragging about what a rich man he was! "Well, you ain't the only one, Brother Pointer," Bertha told him suavely in her mind. "I woke up here one mornin' a day or two ago, and b'lieve it or not, I was rich too—yes, and I still am! What do you think o' that?"

His calling her beautiful had astonished her, and of course it sent her to the kitchen mirror. After a long look she turned away pleased and smiling. The old fellow had two eyes in his head, after all. "Why, Brother Pointer, I'm surprised at you!" she imagined herself saying coquettishly; but her eyes fell before the thought, as they would have fallen before his answering gaze. Such words as those Brother Pointer would not answer; not even to tell her that she had belittled herself.

But she was committed now, not only to Brother Pointer but to herself. Even had she not been powerless against her longing for Jeff, the mere matter of her hurt pride would have made her reckless in meeting the preacher's challenge. Brother Pointer, though of course he did not know it, had only added fuel to the blaze by calling her beautiful. She had never been so called in her life before, and her confidence mounted to the point of danger. Between his visit and the "Christmas doin's" she made occasion to see Jeff every day. It was easy enough; he could use her help and was very grateful for it, though she saw sometimes (and hotly refused to see) that he was surprised at her frequent visits to the school.

Other women were coming now from time to time, which both relieved and irritated Bertha. If Lucy Wilkerson or Mrs. Bartlett or Mrs. Baker came while she was there, it required the utmost restraint of her to be civil; yet she told herself that they could not very well "talk about her," since they themselves were doing the selfsame thing.

When she appeared for the third time bringing a finished costume, Jeff laughed. "Bertha, you don't have to be so conscientious, you know—you needn't make a trip every time you get something done. Just so they're here by that night—that's all that matters."

Bertha was discomposed. She hesitated. "They was some-thin' elst I wanted to ast you about, Mr. Plant. Opal, she says you want her to paint her face—"

"Oh, just a touch of rouge and lip salve, Bertha, nothing fancy. Those colored lights will make her look pale if she doesn't. By the way, though, I'm glad you've come. See if you can't get her to leave her hair alone. The mantle will cover most of it, I know, but those frizzes—"

"I'll talk to her," Bertha said eagerly. "I'll show her the picture again."

"You do that, Bertha. Look, where shall we put the tree? I thought over here, just across from the organ, maybe. What do you think?"

"That'd be fine." Bertha nodded approvingly. "You got you a tree picked out yit, Mr. Plant? I c'd git you one, if you ain't."

Jeff laughed. "What an Amazon! That's man's work, Ber-tha. I'll take a couple of the big boys out with a sled. Thanks just the same, though."

Bertha was disappointed, but she tried again. "Mr. Plant," she began, "I was a-thinkin'—I got all my kids' costumes done already. If'n they's ary young 'un can't git one finished in time—"

Jeff was delighted. "Oh, would you, Bertha, really? I wanted to ask you, but I hated to; you've done so much already. I do want an angel's robe for Molly Pointer. She'll be here that night, and she knows a poem to recite. I've got the stuff and the picture right over here." He brought her some soft white muslin and a length of Chrismas-tree tinsel. "Just make it straight up and down like a nightgown, you know, and trim the neck and sleeves with the tinsel, like this sketch. I've got some more tinsel she can wear for a crown. You're an angel, yourself, Bertha, you really are."

Bertha, trapped, could say nothing in protest, though the last thing she wanted was to make Molly a costume. At least she had wrung out the words she yearned to hear. Whatever praise he gave her she hoarded like gold; it was one more thing to turn over and over in her mind, to whisper to herself at night in bed. Though she departed each time with a sickness at her heart that he had not touched her, she had always these words to answer her inward fear. She knew, by this time, that the other women were talking. She had come into the store yesterday on a gale of female tittering, and it had died down instantly at her approach. She faced them down. "You was there yourselves," her eyes countered theirs. But it seared her.

At home she had to walk warily enough. Both the meals and the housework had suffered to some extent, and Tim, as always, had to be catered to, lest he discharge the vials of his wrath on Clarence. "You goin' plumb dippy about that there Christmas doin's?" he would demand, and then bellow for Clance. When Clance came, he would berate him for anything handy—for not bringing wood, though the box was two-thirds full; for getting a smudge on the kitchen roller towel. If Bertha intervened, he shouted "Shet up! If'n I hear any more outen either one o' you I'll Christmas doin's you, lemme tell you that!" And, cuffing at random any child he could reach—most frequently Ardeth, who was in her high chair and helpless—he would stamp out of the house in disgust, leaving Bertha to soothe the anguished and pick up the pieces. Bertha's heart burned, as always, with impotent rage, but her conscience was too active to permit it release. She had meant so well by the children, and look at her now. "I can't help it," she cried to herself, ashamed. "It ain't a-goin' to be but a little while."

At this point she found it politic to stop thinking. The logical next question, "A little while until what?" she could not answer. She went feverishly back to counting up her words: "You're priceless, Bertha".... "Bertha, you're an angel".... "I don't know what I'd do without you, Bertha." And there were the times he had touched her, the day he had kissed her. Her heart turned over with memory and desire.

She took Opal aside one evening and showed her the picture. "See, Opal, the Virgil Mary ain't got no curls."

"She ain't got hair like mine, neither," Opal said glumly.

"Your'n'd look like that if'n you'd give it half a chanst.

Mr. Plant, he don't want you should frizzle it up thataway."

Opal was lofty. "Mr. Plant! What does he know? It's my hair, ain't it?"

"None o' your sass, young lady. You do as I say, or I'll git him to let somebody elst be in it. You hear me?" And a moment later, as Opal departed, muttering, for the kitchen, she called after her mildly: "Don't pour out that there buttermilk when you git through with it, Opal. My hands is right chapped; I thought maybe I'd soak 'em awhile."

XVI

She made short work of the angel's robe for Molly, but she did not carry it to the schoolhouse until the last possible moment, though she went every day as usual. She wished that she had kept back Opal's costume too. The sight of Opal in the blue mantle had given her her first moment of maternal pride in the girl, and had, moreover, carried with it an obscure comfort. The mantle stilled and burnished Opal, somehow. Bertha told herself that she had never noticed before what pretty eyes Opal had.

On the evening of the entertainment she went early to the schoolhouse, using Molly's costume as an excuse to leave Opal in charge of the house. Jeff and several big boys were already there, working over the final decorations. "Hello, Bertha," he greeted her absently. "Hand me the end of that garland over there, will you?"

The whole front of the little schoolroom was banked and festooned with evergreens, set here and there with a giant red candle or a wreath with a red ribbon bow. The great Christmas tree, decked out in strings of popcorn and cranberries and further embellished with the glittering trinkets Jeff had brought from town, stood across the room from the wheezy

133

little organ, its branches weighted down with little tarletan bags of candy and peanuts. The organ was piled with small packages wrapped in tissue and tied with red and green ribbon. "The bag wouldn't hold 'em all," Jeff explained. "There's a present for everybody, such as it is. How does it look, Bertha? How do you like it?"

"It's jest beautiful, Mr. Plant," said Bertha sincerely.

"If we only get through it without setting the building on fire," Jeff continued, "I'm satisfied. Bud's organized a bucket brigade in case we need it." He sank his voice to a mutter. "My God, will you look at that!" He jerked his head slightly in the direction of the entrance. Bertha turned.

"That" was Mamie Johnson. She was unattended, Hughie being not yet in evidence. Mamie settled herself comfortably, took a fresh stick of gum from her purse, unwrapped it and leaned back with a loud sigh of satisfaction. Her dress, of sleazy imitation velvet, was violently green—perhaps in celebration of Christmas, for she had piled outrage upon the outrage of her hair by attaching to it a cluster of bright scarlet artificial flowers. Brother Pointer, arriving with Molly in tow a few minutes later, blinked rapidly several times as he caught sight of her. "You run on up yander to the platform, honey," he directed, urging Molly ahead of him, "where Mr. Plant is. He'll tell you where to go.... Howdy, Mis' Johnson," he added hurriedly as Molly reluctantly obeyed him, her fascinated backward gaze fixed on Mamie's topknot.

Mamie's only acknowledgement of his greeting was a brief cessation in the motion of her jaws. Brother Pointer, however, had not waited for even this response. He had moved on to the front of the room and now knelt beside one of the little desks, praying. Mamie's ruminative expression became truculent. Her chewing approached the frenetic, and she displayed an impressive array of large, square, steadily grinding teeth. Bertha, from the opposite direction, noted Brother Pointer's prayerful attitude with much the same distaste. "He's a-prayin' either at me or at that Mame Johnson. Both of us, maybe. It's all the same to him." Brother

Pointer finished his prayer and rose, making his way to the platform where they stood. "Howdy, Mr. Plant. Howdy, boys. Howdy, Mis' Mallory." He turned to face Jeff. "I was jest a-wonderin', Mr. Plant, if'n you wouldn't want me to talk first, afore the entertainment gits started."

"Why, yes, Brother Pointer, if you think so. We're always glad to hear you. You know that."

"I ain't aimin' to preach no regular sermon," Brother Pointer hastened to assure him. "I jest thought, long's the people's all gathered together, the good Lord wouldn't want me to miss a chanst to tell 'em the glad tidin's oncet agin." He paused. "That there pore Mis' Johnson's here a'ready. Maybe this here's the night He'll lead her home." His glance took in Bertha. "Mr. Plant was a-tellin' me you made my Molly a dress, Mis' Mallory," he said. "I thank you kindly."

"You're welcome," Bertha forced herself to say. Mamie Johnson indeed! It was not Mamie Johnson he would be preaching at. One way or another he always had to put in his oar! Here she'd just been about to ask Mr. Plant about his book, and now it was too late, the room was filling. Her own family, all but Clance, had arrived. Bertha began to worry at once; where was he? But then he came in, glowering, and sat down.

She relaxed with a sigh and beckoned the other children. "You git on up here and do like Mr. Plant says," she directed. He'll tell you when it's time fer you to git dressed."

The children, their eyes bright and eager, their breath coming short, were only too willing to be docile and obey. "Now don't you git skeered, Clovis, when it comes time to sing," Bertha admonished the nervous little boy. "You sung it fine fer me last night at home. You sing it like that tonight and you'll do fine."

She noted that Opal's hair was defiantly frizzed. Well, there was nothing to do about it now, and no use getting worked up. Unable any longer to delay, she left the platform and sat down between her husband and the scowling Clarence. She saw Bud Wilkerson enter with Lucy and the children, and there came the Bakers and their twelve-year-old daughter Lily, with three or four younger children trailing behind. "Looks like they's a-goin' to be a right good crowd," she thought. "Yes, and there comes that Hughie Conroy after all." She watched young Conroy with hard and hostile eyes. "If'n it's Opal you're a-lookin' fer," she told him mentally as his bold blue eyes went searching round the room, "you might jest as well set down and say your prayers. This here's one night you ain't a-goin' to come near her."

Brother Pointer, on the platform, opened his Bible. "Except a corn of wheat—" He cleared his throat, raising his voice a little. "Except a corn of wheat fall into the ground and die, it abideth alone; but if it die it bringeth forth much fruit."

Bertha fidgeted. What kind of talk was that? "If God written that there Bible, it looks like He'd 'a' knowed corn and wheat ain't nothin' alike. Even Ardeth'd know better'n to say 'a corn o' wheat.' " She paid Brother Pointer no further close attention as he set forth the glory of sacrifice, beyond noticing that it sounded much the same as what he had told her that last day at the farm, about God taking trouble and loss and turning them into riches. She was not in the mood for sermons, and she would not hear; so she fixed her uneasy mind on the illogical phrase, letting her irritation fill her to the exclusion of all else. "Anybody knows wheat can't come up unlest you plant it, nor corn neither, but seems to me like they might make up their minds which one they're a-talkin' about."

She tried to relax and sit still, but a nervous unease was upon her. She sighed with relief as he finished and Molly, an engaging angel in the long white robe and a little tinsel halo, came out on the platform to "say her piece" about the Babe of Christmas:

> "Away in a manger,
> No crib for He bed,
> The litto Lord Yedus—"

Again, as always, Molly's sweet fearlessness struck on her

naked heart. She had had six children, but never one like this; yet Brother Pointer would have her believe God loved her!

The program moved on its way without mishap. The children sang several carols with varying degrees of tunefulness, and a number of soap-sleek little girls and boys squeaked out recitations. The tableaux, most of whose participants were the older pupils, had been saved for the finale. As the first of them was announced, Clarence suddenly rose and bolted out of the room. Bertha made a clutch at him, but he escaped her.

Tim turned upon her a brow of thunder. "What's that there young devil up to now?" he demanded. Bertha, miserable, shook her head. "I'll settle his hash when I git him home tonight," Tim promised her, and turned his attention back to the entertainment

Bertha, cold and sick with apprehension, could not look at the tableau, though Daisy, Woodrow and Ardeth all had part in it. The scene was a presentation of Christmas Eve, with children sitting around a fireplace hung with stockings and decked with holly while their mother, personified by Daisy, read them the Christmas story from the Bible. Bertha, look where she might, could see nothing at all but Clarence. Even the wonder of the colored lights left her unmoved, although a sigh of enchantment swept through the audience at the sight, and even Mamie Johnson stopped chewing her gum.

Several other tableaux followed in rapid succession, and still he had not reappeared. Bertha's state of mind was approaching panic. She found it almost impossible to keep her seat. There was not much time left now; if he didn't come......

The final tableau, that in which Opal figured as the Virgin, with Clovis singing *Gesu Bambino* behind the scenes, was about to appear. Bertha had worried herself into a frenzy about Clovis' possible stage fright, but she had altogether forgotten him now.

The improvised curtain went up. Jeff played a chord or

two on the organ. One of the big boys, in a hidden recess, touched off the red tableau powder, and the Nativity scene glowed forth in its indestructible magic, bewitching the unsophisticated audience to breathlessness. Jeff lifted a hand to Clovis behind the scenes, and the little boy's timid treble arose and faltered. Suddenly, outside the window behind the evergreens, the air was picked up by a violin. Clovis, heartened by the sound, overcame his fear and sang freely, delicately, beautifully, the imperfections of his rendition masked by the almost unbearably sweet accompaniment from without. Bertha caught her breath, paling. Tim stiffened. People all over the room stirred and looked at each other, their lips parted. Brother Pointer sat like one in a trance, his eyes uplifted as to the choiring of angels. And indeed there was an unearthly quality in the obbligato, which, as soon as Clovis had recovered himself, strayed from the melody to variation after variation, wild, wandering, awe-stricken, pleading. Even the boys and girls in the group around the Manger, though they maintained their positions, were shaken. Their faces, Opal's too, in the repeated flares of ruby light were swept with innocent wonder.

Bertha's heart thudded in her throat. How could he play like that, with no one to teach him or help him? Why could he not have said he was going to play? Her chest ached with mingled pain and happiness. Surely Tim could not punish him for this.

The last of the flares died down. The curtain fell. Bud Wilkerson, augmented fore and aft with stuffed-in pillows, burst forth with a merry shout to deliver the presents. Jeff, moving out to help him, caught Bertha's eye. "You see," his look said, as plainly as if he had spoken.

Bertha did see, and agony mounted within her. What did he expect her to do? There was nothing she could do, not though Clarence had been the angel Israfel in person. She was tied hand and foot, and Mr. Plant, of all people, ought to know it. How could he blame her even with a look?

The audience, having caught its breath after the spectacle, was gay. Children and adults alike received their gifts with startled delight. A few of them had brought gifts in return. Lily Baker, beaming, her homely little face alight with benevolence, presented Jeff with a cravat whose colors rivaled a Catalina sunset for brilliance and variety. "It cost a dollar, Mr. Plant. It shore is shiny."

"It certainly is, Lily. Thank you ever so much." Jeff smilingly took off the tie he was wearing and replaced it with the satin horror. "I'll wear it as long as it lasts, and then I'll put it away to remember you by."

Lily, abashed, backed away smiling shyly. Jeff, passing Bertha, touched her shoulder lightly. "Having fun, Bertha?" But before she could answer he was gone again, shouting. "Bud! Hey, Bud, Christmas present for Santa Claus."

Wilkerson opened the package and emitted a whoop of delight. "I be dogged if'n it ain't fishin' tackle!" he cried, turning to his doubtfully smiling wife to exhibit his prize. "Ain't that there the prettiest fly you ever seen, Lucy? Shore is nice of you, Mr. Plant."

Mamie Johnson, somewhat hesitantly presented by Bud with a package containing handkerchiefs, stopped chewing and looked a little wild, but bobbed acknowledgement. Bertha found in her package a little framed photograph of the Nativity scene with Opal in the center, snapped by Jeff's kodak in secret a few days before. For a moment she was diverted from her persistent anxiety about Clarence and Tim, and even from the thought of the way Jeff had looked at her. But as the party broke up her dread returned, and she talked placatingly to Tim all the way home.

Opal trailed along behind them, oddly silent. At the door she darted in ahead of them, her hand against her mouth. Bertha, following her through the house to the kitchen door, heard her just outside it, retching. "Opal!" she called. "What's the matter with you? You sick?"

Opal bent forward in another spasm. "I'm sick at my stomach," she gasped as her mother set a capable hand against her forehead.

"There," Bertha said at last. "I reckon you ben a-doin' too much; you're tired out. Go on to bed and git some sleep.

You'll feel better in the mornin'."

Opal laughed, returning her anxious look with a defiant sneer. "I reckon I'll be worse before I'm better," she said pointedly.

Bertha's knees gave under her. Her face went white. She set her hands hard on the girl's shoulders, searching her face with dread and rising certainty. "You mean," she whispered, "you mean—"

"Yes, I mean!" Opal mocked her, wrenching herself away. "'Tain't nothin' to you as fer as I c'n see. It's ben nothin' but Clance, Clance, Clance with you ever senst I c'n remember." She backed slowly away, obviously frightened but covering her apprehension with bravado. "What you lookin' at me that way fer? It's kind o' late fer you to be takin' a interest, ain't it?"

XVII

Bertha, her knees like water, started into the bedroom where Tim had gone before her, but bethought herself in time of Opal's danger and ordered the girl into the enclosed woodshed that adjoined the kitchen. "You stay in here till I come let you out," she commanded.

"I want to go to bed," said Opal sullenly. "I'm sleepy."

Without a word Bertha turned and left her, coming back with a quilt, a blanket and a small pillow. These she dropped on the floor of the shed, without speaking. She shut the door upon Opal, turned the key in the padlock, took it out and dropped it into her bosom. She then went stoically to confront her husband. "You better put your clo'es back on and go after the preacher," she told him dully. "Opal's in trouble."

Tim's jaw fell. He hauled up his trousers, which he had been removing, and yanked the belt from them as he did so. The children, electrified, inched their way in to watch. "Where's she at?" Tim snarled, lowering his head like a bull.

"You'll not tech her," Bertha told him calmly. "You'll not lay as much as a finger on her and her the way she is, not unless you want to kill me first." She laid a restraining hand upon Clarence, who had leaped at once to her side. "It's that there Hughie Conroy, I reckon. Go git him."

"I'll git him all right." Tim fumbled at his trouser buttons. "And when I git aholt of him—"

Bertha laughed harshly. "I don't reckon I'd shoot him if I was you, not till after we git him married to Opal."

"Shoot him?" Tim's upper lip lifted, his yellow fangs gleaming like a wild animal's. "With good clean bullets for good clean squirrels?"

Daisy and Ardeth, terrified, trembled and whimpered at his tone. Daisy began to cry.

"I won't shoot him," Tim said, reaching for his coat. "I'll slit him from head to hindquarters, that's what I'll do. I'll slit him up and down like a God-damned shoat."

Daisy screamed. His heavy hand shot out and sent her spinning against the wall.

"I can jest see you a-doin' it," Bertha retorted as she helped the half-stunned child to her staggering feet. "Go on to bed now, Daisy, and the rest of you too. This here ain't no place fer young 'uns." She turned back to Tim. "You're mighty biggety, ain't you, when it comes to beatin' up on a helpless little girl like Opal or Daisy? I wisht I was as safe from the devil in hell as Hughie Conroy is from you. You ain't got the spunk to split a flea when you git right down to it! Now will you go git that preacher and that boy, or do you want I should go after 'em myself?"

She towered over him, menace in every line of her powerful frame. Tim stared at her amazed in the midst of his fury, for he did not realize that this was the first time in all their experience that Bertha had been confronted by a situation that could not be turned against Clarence. For a moment he was quite without power to speak.

It was neither of them, but Clarence, who broke the tense silence. "I'll git 'em fer you, Ma," he said, and was gone before she could stop him. She turned back to Tim and gave him a searching look. The relief in his eyes was unmistakable, and before the contempt in hers he shrank a little, turning half away.

"Yes, I would if'n I was you," Bertha began, and, as with her first word he bolted into the bedroom, she shouted after him, "I'd go crawl in a hole and never come out agin!"

But there was no time now to seek revenge on Tim. She

was all alarm for Clarence, who might or might not have sense enough to go first for the preacher and some other man to help him. Would he perhaps attack Hughie alone like a panther in the night, and possibly kill or be killed? There was no knowing. "I wisht Mr. Plant was here," she thought nervously, forgetting for the moment Opal's shame and the humiliation of his knowledge of it.

A burned-out log fell down within the stove, and Bertha jumped. "I better see about Opal," she thought dully, and went to unlock the door of the kitchen shed. Opal lay on her pallet, sleeping sweetly. She had enfolded herself again in the blue mantle, but the hood had fallen away from her matted curls. Bertha stood there looking down at her with fresh pain. How could Opal accuse her of not caring what happened to anybody but Clarence, when she had come so near to killing Mamie Johnson just for telling the girl Hughie Conroy's name? "Opal never did have no sense," she told herself hotly. "A pretty-lookin' thing she is now, ain't she? Sleepin' as peaceful as a coon in winter. Don't make no differ'nce to her if'n she's brung her folks to shame. She's a fine one to be pickin' other folks to pieces."

But she knew that this was guilt's own self-deception. Opal had spoken truly; it was of herself Bertha had been thinking when she set out for Milltown; the disgrace, the scalding shame before the community and Mr. Plant. Nothing of this could matter to her now. It was all within herself, the disgrace and the shame. She was as guilty as Opal, for she had failed her. "They'll come a time when you can't help them childern no more," Brother Pointer had said. Well, now that time had come so far as Opal was concerned.

Yet even in this moment Bertha did not see how she could have done otherwise and survived. Until Mr. Plant's arrival, Clarence had been all that kept her alive and willing to live.

She heard a quick rapping at the kitchen door. Locking the shed door behind her, she went to answer it. Jeff Plant stood there, his eyes compassionate. "Let me in, Bertha," he said quietly. "Clance just told me about it, and I thought I'd better come. Don't worry, he's got the doctor with him, and they'll get Brother Pointer before they go to Milltown."

Bertha said nothing. Jeff entered and took off his overcoat. "Take it easy, Bertha. We'll get you through it somehow. Where is Tim?"

"He's went to bed, I reckon," Bertha replied, her somber eyes fixed hard on the schoolmaster's face.

Jeff drew up a chair for her and seated himself. "Bertha, I can't begin to tell you how sorry I am. I did try once to get hold of Hughie and talk to him—"

She nodded. "It ain't no fault o' yourn, Mr. Plant. You done all you could."

"I'm not so sure. I did all I thought I could, but—"

"They wasn't nothin' could 'a' stopped Opal after that there boy come," Bertha continued tonelessly. "She ain't a-feelin' bad about it even now. She went right to sleep just like nothin' at all was the matter. I reckon she thinks she's a-spitin' me, or somethin'." A long shuddering sigh escaped her.

"They can't be married tonight," Jeff went on, "because they'll have to go to town for the license, but we won't let Hughie out of our sight till it's over. We'll have him at the license bureau as soon as it's open in the morning. Opal will have to appear too, I suppose. She's not too ill to get to town, is she?"

"I reckon Opal'll manage all right." Bertha moistened her dry lips, feeling a dull surprise that she had thought nothing of a marriage license. They sat for a while in silence, the old clock on the cupboard ticking the time away. Jeff motioned with his head toward the bedroom door. "He didn't hurt Opal, did he?"

Bertha shook her head. "He was a-goin' to, but I stopped him. I wouldn't let him. He hit Daisy a awful lick, though, before I seen what he was at."

"Daisy? What for?"

"She was a-cryin'," Bertha explained. "He skeered her." She glanced wearily at the clock. "Seems like they ain't never goin' to git here, don't it?"

"It always seems like that when you're waiting for something. Why don't you go and lie down a little while, Bertha? I'll call you when they come."

"I ain't tired," she answered, and added with an effort, "It was mighty nice in you, Mr. Plant, to come right over."

"Nice in me! For God's sake, Bertha, we're friends, aren't we?"

Bertha looked at him and quivered, but said nothing. There was nothing she could say without betraying herself. It would be nice, she thought, if Mr. Plant could know what it meant to her to have him sharing her vigil, apparently uninfluenced by Opal's shame to the least deviation from his steady loyalty. It would be almost enough to ease her of her pain. Perhaps, in that clairvoyant way of his, he knew it; but if he did not, there was no way she could tell him.

The clock struck one before the shuffle of feet was heard without. The male group entered wordlessly, Clarence black and beetling, Hughie sullen and silent, his yellow hair still rumpled from his pillow and straggling out from under his woollen cap. Bud Wilkerson, surprisingly among those present, his good-natured face sheepish with embarrassment, kept his gaze sedulously on the floor. Dr. Brumbaugh, having duly performed the duty at hand, took leave at once. "I reckon there's enough of you here to look after things," he said. "But call me again if you need me. Good night, all."

Brother Pointer, his face a mask of misery, pulled up a chair. "Berthy—"

Bertha shook her head violently. "Don't you talk to me now, Brother Pointer, I can't stand it. I ain't in no humor to hear no preacher talk."

Brother Pointer, seeing the white line about her lips, fell silent. Bertha turned to look for Clarence. "Clance, you better—"

"Lemme alone. I'm a-goin' to bed," said the boy, and made his word good with no further ado.

An uncomfortable silence fell. Bertha broke it at last. "I'm much obliged to you all fer comin' over," she said mechanically.

They made sounds of deprecatory acknowledgement, and Bertha became acutely aware of Tim snoring in the bedroom. Shame and contempt filled her body from head to foot, but she knew that anything said or done would but make matters worse. The disgrace that lay on her now could hardly be deepened whatever Tim did.

She sat on, therefore, in silence, the whole world black and meaningless about her. When she tried to take comfort in knowing Jeff was there, she felt only an increased bleakness and a strange, nagging nausea. Somehow she had faced him tonight, but she felt that she could never meet his eyes by day.

Brother Pointer at last rose and excused himself. "I'll be gittin' on home, I reckon. I don't like fer Molly to be down yander by herself no longer. You let me know when you're ready fer me tomorrer, Mr. Plant."

"That's right, Brother Pointer. Get yourself some sleep."

Brother Pointer turned to Bertha. "Good-night, Berthy," he said courteously, but she did not answer.

The silence fell again when he had gone. "I believe I'll make some coffee," Jeff said at last. "You could use some, couldn't you, Bud?"

Bud nodded, and Jeff turned to the scowling culprit, who sat near the kitchen door, unmoving. Hughie had not removed his cap and nobody had offered to take it from him. It was pulled down now as far over his eyes as possible, in an evident effort to discourage questioning. "Hughie, how about you? Would you like to have a cup of coffee?"

Hughie shifted in his chair. "It don't make no differ'nce to me."

Jeff made the coffee and Bud and Hughie accepted it, but Bertha refused. "I couldn't swaller it, Mr. Plant, but thanks jest the same."

He looked at her anxiously. "Why don't you go to bed, Bertha? You can't do any good just sitting here and wearing yourself out. You're white as a sheet right now."

She shook her head. Jeff, pouring himself a cup of coffee and glancing in Hughie's direction as he did so, spoke in a lowered tone to Wilkerson. "Have any trouble in Milltown?"

Bud shook his head. "Naw. Naw, he come all right."

"How'd they happen to get hold of you?"

Bud grinned and made an attempt to hide behind his cup. "I 'uz already there," he admitted sheepishly.

"Oh, for God's sake," Jeff said, startled. He glanced at Bertha, but if she had heard at all she gave no sign. He turned his head, listening. "Somebody's coming, I think."

Bud tweaked the curtain aside and looked out the window. "Jesus!" he exclaimed, "I got to go!" He set down the cup with a clatter and seized his cap, diving without ceremony through the next room and out by the front door.

"What the devil?" Jeff began, looking at Bertha, whose blank expression did not change in the least, even at the loud knock that resounded through the house a moment later. Jeff opened the door and blinked incredulously. Mamie Johnson stood there, wearing a man's overcoat and a hat like a spraying fountain of green ostrich plumes. She carried a stout umbrella in one hand and held the other clenched over something concealed from view. She said nothing, but chewed her gum with vigor.

"Did you want to see Hughie?" Jeff inquired at length, a little disconcerted by her silence and the steadiness of her gaze.

Mamie nodded. Hughie, on hearing his name spoken, dropped his tilted chair to the floor with a bang and turned to look. "You go back home," he commanded his aunt, with decision. "I ain't no baby. I know what I'm a-doin'. Go on home, you hear me?"

Mamie shifted her gaze to him, her jaws moving tentatively.

"You hear me?" he shouted again. "You git on back home!"

But Mamie had made up her mind; she pushed her way in. Jeff cast an appalled and helpless glance at Bertha, who had apparently turned altogether to stone. Mamie paid no attention to either Jeff or her hostess; she put her umbrella down on a chair and reached into the pocket of her overcoat, drawing out an unopened package of gum. Laying it placatingly on the table at Hughie's side, she took off her coat and sat down placidly.

"Will you—would you like a cup of coffee?" Jeff ventured at last, with another apprehensive glance in Bertha's direction.

Apparently Mamie, though she did not speak, had no objection. Jeff poured it for her and sat down helplessly. Hughie had pulled his cap still farther down and elevated his feet to the rungs of a vacant kitchen chair. To all appearances he had gone to sleep.

Mamie drank her coffee serenely, set down the empty cup and took off her hat. Her eyes darted here and there about the room, at length perceiving an army cot in a corner. To this she repaired without any hesitation, taking off her shoes and setting them side by side beneath its edge. She had kept her left hand clenched on its contents throughout, but now she laid the thing, a rounded stone of about the size of an egg, on the floor beside her shoes; having done so, she lay down upon the cot, turned her back, hitched herself into a comfortable position, and slept.

Jeff gasped and looked appealingly at Bertha, but Bertha would neither meet his gaze nor speak. As Mamie emitted a faintly whistling snore, he tried again. "What do you suppose she was going to do with that rock? Was she out to protect her one ram lamb, or did she intend it for Bud?"

Still Bertha was silent. He carried his chair to her side, and spoke to her gently. "Bertha, I want to help you, you know that? You know I'm your friend? You mean a lot to me."

She looked at him at last, but her eyes fell. A little encouraged, he took her hand in his. "Try not to take it so hard, Bertha. It isn't really the end of the world, you know. Hughie's a good worker, I'll say that for him, and as for Opal—well, nearly all the girls around here get married like this—"

Bertha flinched. "I never got married no sech a way, Mr. Plant."

"Bertha, my God, no! Of course you didn't; I didn't mean to say—"

"Ner my mammy never got married no sech a way, ner

neither did hern. Opal'll be the first one." She turned away. She was hurt to the heart, and she did not quite know why. Mr. Plant meant well, he was always kind, he had been kinder than ever all this black night. While Tim snored placidly and forgot their shame, Mr. Plant sat here patiently beside her, trying and trying and trying his best to help. Yet he did not help, Bertha knew in desperation. There was no comfort for her in his nearness.

She controlled herself to answer him somehow. "Hadn't you better go home and get some sleep?"

He hesitated. "I'll go, of course, Bertha, if you want me to."

"I think—I think maybe you better," she said faintly.

"Will you be all right?" He indicated Mamie. "She might get rough, you know, and if she does—"

"She'll wisht she hadn't," said Bertha for all reply.

Jeff smiled. "That sounds more like you. Well, if you're sure. I'll be back in the morning, of course." She nodded, and he rose and put on his coat. "Try to take it easier, Bertha. It'll all come out in the wash."

Bertha did not rise to go with him to the door. She tried to say, at least, "Good-bye, Mr. Plant," and to thank him again for his kindness, but words would not come. Long after the kitchen door had closed behind him she sat on motionless, not even rising to replenish the fire. Across from her on the cot Mamie Johnson snored gently, and Hughie, obviously asleep though sitting almost upright, made no impression on her consciousness. She had forgotten that Opal still lay in the shed, and no sound of unease came thence to remind her.

The mandatory wedding took place in the early afternoon of the next day; the family, Jeff and Mamie Johnson were the only witnesses. Opal had entirely recovered her aplomb and smirked with satisfaction and triumph. She was coquettish with Hughie, no whit disturbed by the glum silence with which he met her wheedlings.

Bertha had roused herself enough by morning to waken Tim and compel him to put in an appearance. He sat stolid and silent throughout the proceedings, his eyes on Bertha's forbidding face. The children, excited but afraid to betray it in the face of their elders' tense silence, looked at each other and then, fascinated, at Opal. Jeff was for some reason nervous and ill at ease; from time to time he looked at his watch and frowned.

Brother Pointer performed the ceremony with sorrowful gravity. " 'Tain't never too late," he told the erring couple, "fer us pore sinnin' human critters to mend our ways and look to the Lord fer mercy. If'n you're truly sorry fer what you done, ast His fergiveness and you'll git it. Let us pray."

The rites finally over, the bridal couple and Mamie put on their wraps to depart. Bertha got to her feet, alarmed. "Whereabouts do you think you're a-goin', Opal?" she demanded.

Hughie answered for his bride, with a triumphant leer. "We're a-goin' down to Aunt Mame's, o' course. Where elst is they fer us to go to?"

Bertha breathed hard. "Opal she ain't a-goin' down to your Aunt Mame's, not by a jug full." She turned upon Opal. "You take off that there coat, young lady, and stay here where you belong, or I'll—"

Opal laughed and thrust her arm through Mamie's. Mamie, who at Bertha's word had clamped a hard upper jaw down on her gum and tightened her fists, relaxed and nodded. Jeff, seeing Bertha's sudden ghastly pallor, did what he could. "Bertha, maybe Lucy Wilkerson or Mrs. Baker would take them in for a while, till they know what they want to do. Let me go down and—"

Hughie was offended. "If'n my Aunt Mame ain't good enought fer Opal—"

"Anything that gits me outen this here house fer oncet and all is good enought fer me," Opal put in airily. "Come on, Hughie." She made for the door, dragging Mamie with her. Bertha took an agitated step forward, but Jeff restrained her. "You may as well give her her head for the time being, Bertha. She'll be glad enough to come home in a few days—"

"Yes, I will—not!" Opal's jeering voice, heady with new

authority, came back through the half-closed door. "Fat chanst! Come on, Hughie. I reckon our lives is our own from now on, ain't they?"

"You mighty right, they air," Hughie bellowed back. He jammed his cap on his head and cast a jaunty look backward at the stricken company. "Well, happy Noo Year," he added blithely.

Tim had not moved or spoken, but now he rose and, still without a word, put on his cap and mackinaw and left the house. Brother Pointer departed a few moments later, and Jeff, with a final glance at his watch, turned back to Bertha after seeing the old preacher to the door. "Wrap up the children for me, Bertha; I'm taking them over to Wilkersons' for the day. You need a rest, and Lucy said bring them along. They'll stay for supper, so you won't have to worry about that. Bud'll bring them home in the sleigh before their bedtime." As Bertha hesitated he turned to Daisy. "You get the things for all of you, won't you, Daisy? Your mother's tired out. She's got to take a rest."

Clarence, at the first word of this proposal, had seized his things and disappeared from the scene. The other children, immediately eager at the prospect of detailing to the Wilkerson children the excitement of the day, were soon bundled into their wraps and following the teacher down the snowy road.

XVIII

They were gone. It was over. Bertha rose heavily and piled the coffee cups and the other dishes on the table ready for washing. She filled the dishpan from the steaming teakettle, tempered the water with a dipperful of cold, got out soap and cloth and towels, and dropped a pile of cutlery into the pan. Then, abruptly, she found that she could not go on. She paced the length of the kitchen a time or two, as she might have done in looking for something mislaid. She sat down. She rose again. She could not rest. She could not work. "I can't even live, seems like," she thought, her breath catching.

It was funny, she thought, how fast the time went by. According to the clock, it was an hour since all of them had left her; and the clock must be right, for there was the whistle of the early afternoon train, sounding thin and far across the snow. "You wouldn't think that there deepot was two miles off," thought Bertha.

She wished that she had begged Jeff to stay a while. "It ain't no wonder he didn't, though, the way I acted. There he set and set, a-tryin' to talk to me nice, and I jest set there like a bump on a log. I wisht he was here now, though. I wisht I c'd see him."

Perhaps she could see him. Perhaps she could go to him. It was Saturday. He was sure to be at home in such weather as this. And this time, if he asked her in, she would go. She had two books to return; that would be an excuse. If she could sit with him there by the fire a while—

True, he had sat with her last night for more than a while, and it had seemed to do her little good. His presence had been comforting, but his words—"He talked as nice as anybody could," she argued. "And he said—he told me he thought a lot of me, too."

But she could not escape the pricking thorn, the indeterminate something that had hurt her. For this reason as much as any other, she longed to see him again, to search his eyes, to reassure herself that nothing was wrong. "They couldn't be nothin' wrong," she contended desperately.

It would do her good, anyhow, to get out of doors. Nobody would see her. Nobody would be out. The skies were laden with more snow ready to fall. The light outside the window, at one o'clock, was full of the purple of dusk. It was bitter cold. She would have to wrap up well.

She banked the kitchen fire, put on a heavy sweater and then her coat, and wrapped her head and half her face in a shawl, then buckled heavy arctics over her shoes. She had no gloves, but the coat had big deep pockets. She was outside before she remembered the books, but she recalled them in time to go back and get them.

The deep snow, broken only by a few tracks, made progress slow and very difficult. Nearly half an hour had passed before she came within sight of the Bend. Her wraps were still inadequate to such cold; she was chilled and shivering from head to foot. She remembered, with a sort of angry incredulity, the hammering heat of last July and August. "Seems like it's always got to be one or the other," she thought wearily.

As she had foreseen, she was the only one abroad. The whole world might have been empty of life for all Bertha could see. Over her head the purple snow-clouds billowed, so low that they seemed to her to be pushing her down. Fences and farm buildings looked unfamiliar and forbidding, smoothed and rounded under the white weight of

snow. She remembered a poem she had read in one of Jeff's
books:

> O the long and dreary winter!
> O the cold and cruel winter!
> Ever thicker, thicker, thicker
> Froze the ice on lake and river.
> Ever deeper, deeper, deeper
> Fell the snow o'er all the landscape—

"Yes, and it's a-goin' to fall deeper yit," she muttered.
"This here ain't all it's a-goin' to snow, not by a long shot."

She paused to get her breath. In the near distance was the
teacher's cabin, half hidden by drifted snow. But the doorstep and a path had been shoveled clean, and the snow shovel
still leaned against the front wall. She saw Jeff come out,
smiling. He was not alone. There was a woman with him.

The blood rushed to Bertha's head and away again. "I
knowed it," she said aloud, her body shaking. "I knowed it
all the time, didn't I? I knowed he was as good as married
a'ready."

She could not doubt that the woman was his "girl", his
Claire, who was "wonderful"....so wonderful that while she
was in the world he could not see anybody else. She must
have come on that train, the one that whistled.

She heard the girl suddenly laugh, and her knees buckled.
She sank down in the snow on a fallen tree, the books rolling
from her grasp into a nearby drift. She tried not to look
again, lest they should become aware of her nearness, but she
could not help looking, and when she did she saw Jeff catch
the girl to him and hold her close in a prolonged embrace.
When it broke at last, they disappeared around the corner of
the shack hand in hand, Jeff picking up the snow shovel on
the way.

They were gone, but she saw them still. She would always
see them. The picture of that embrace was printed in lightning on her suffering mind; it was all she had left her now,
for ever and ever. She was sitting here in the snow slowly

freezing to death, but she need not move, because she was dead even now. A woman, a strange woman, a woman she had never seen before, had come to Weary Water, stepped off the train and destroyed her.

From some far recess in the back of her mind, words came to Bertha, slowly, one at a time. Brother Pointer's words, the Bible's: "Except a corn of wheat fall into the ground and die, it abideth alone; but if it die it bringeth forth much fruit."

Much fruit? Much fruit? What fruit was there for her, though she were seven times dead? Brother Pointer had said the words to her, she knew. But what did they mean, and why did she think of them now?

Time passed. Bertha's feet and ankles were numb; her hands were blocks of ice and heavy as stone. "But if it die it bringeth forth much fruit," her memory insisted. It must mean something. It had to. All existence for Bertha had drawn itself together into a hard knot that only these words could untie. Not that it mattered if it were never untied. She had nothing left in the world but her love for Clarence, and much good that would do him. Much good it had ever done him.

But her numbing faculties roused at the thought of him. Her mind cleared a little. She began to see. Perhaps the words meant that if she should die and be put underground "like that there corn o' wheat, as they call it," Clance could go away. He could get away from Tim and go to town, and maybe, as Mr. Plant had said, somebody would help him with his music.

The more she thought of it, the likelier it seemed. Well, that was easy enough. She had only to keep on sitting here and freezing. "I might as well," she thought dully. "Mr. Plant—"

She shuddered violently and to the bone. She could not stop. Her teeth chattered. Then the chill left her as abruptly as it had come; she was no longer cold at all, but only drowsy.

Time passed. Far down the road the soft, strenuous sound of horses' hooves pushing against the snow came dimly to her ears, but she did not stir. "Somebody's a-comin'," she thought, but it meant nothing. Her lethargy was too great for alarm to penetrate; it did not occur to her to wonder what people would think. Even when a startled voice cried "Whoa!" and the team and sleigh halted, she was not roused, did not even turn her head.

Bud Wilkerson, swathed to the ears, sprang out and hurried toward her. "Mis' Mallory! What on airth air you a-doin' out here in this awful cold?"

But at close sight of her face he stopped, aghast. "Aw, now, Mis' Mallory, don't you take it so hard. Opal, she'll be all right in jest a little while."

It was just what Jeff had said, but it sounded different. It brought the tears to her eyes. Bud sat down beside her. "Aw, now, Mis' Mallory, don't you take on like that. Jest look at them pore hands o' yourn; why, they're plumb froze." He took off his mittens and chafed them between his own. "Come on, le's us go git in the sleigh and go home where it's warm. I'm plumb skeered to leave you out here by yourself any longer." He looked at her anxiously. "You pore girl you, why, you're a-freezin' to death!" he cried helplessly.

Bertha's chin trembled, and two tears crept from her eyes, hardening instantly on her cheeks. Bud scraped them away, his hand tender as a woman's. "Now don't you cry and spile them pretty eyes. You come on now, honey, and let Bud take you home."

Bertha, for only answer, broke and sobbed. Bud put his arms around her and hugged her to him. "I reckon you c'n cry if you want to," he said defiantly to nothing, patting her back. "Now then. Now then."

Neither of them noticed the slight crackle of the crusted snow as Clarence Mallory, black-browed and menacing, emerged from the thicket behind them and halted as if glued there. "Honey," Bud went on, thickly, "you pore girl you—" He lifted her face in one of his hands and kissed her. Bertha clung to him, comforted by his nearness. "Now then," he murmured against her icy cheek. "It ain't that bad. It ain't—"

A strangled sound broke from somewhere behind them, and Bertha's shut eyes flew open, seeing Clarence. The sword of her single true motherhood stabbed her awake; she tore herself from Bud's grasp, crying eagerly, "Clance!"

But Clarence turned and fled, without a backward look. "Clance! Clance!" she called after him shrilly, stumbling toward him. "Clance! You wait! You wait fer Maw a minute!"

He paid her no heed. "Clance, wait jest a minute! Lemme tell you how it was!" She sobbed aloud. "Here's how it was, Clance, here's how it was! I never—"

He dodged into a thicket, out of sight. Bertha stopped and stood staring after him, her hands at her sides. A dazzle of dark spots danced before her eyes.

Bud came to her, after a moment, and took her hands. "Le's us go home, Mis' Mallory," he said gently. "Come on. Le's us go home now where it's warm."

She let him lead her toward the sleigh, then remembered the books. "Them books—I was a-takin'—Mr. Plant—"

"I'll git 'em," Bud said. "I'll put 'em on the step. You go on and git in the sleigh and cover up."

But she was quite helpless to get into the sleigh. He found her standing beside it and helped her in. "I got to stop by Baker's jest a minute," he said as he picked up the reins. "I tole Mr. Baker I'd put some freight on the train fer 'im, bein's I'm out anyway. You better come in there with me and git some coffee."

Bertha looked at him piteously, and he soothed her. "Jest don't feel like it, do you? You needn't to. You set out here all covered up nice and warm, and I'll be right back." They were approaching Baker's, and he slowed. "You be all right?" he asked her anxiously.

Bertha nodded. He stopped the sleigh and got out, first tucking the laprobe carefully about her. Tears came again to Bertha's eyes at his kindness. He patted her gently. "I ain't goin' to be but a minute. I'm late now." He sprinted toward the house.

She heard the far whistle of the late afternoon train. "He

ain't a-goin' to make it. I kep' him too long. I wisht he hadn't a-found me. I wisht I'd 'a' froze. Now I got to do it some other way."

For Clarence, she was sure, would never listen. He would never forgive her what he thought he had seen. Bertha knew well that, alone of all the world, she escaped his contempt, though she could not win his love; this was too much, he would never respect her again. And he would be right in refusing, she told herself bitterly. She had done no wrong so far as Bud was concerned. What she might have done, had it been Jeff, was another matter.

The train whistled nearer. Bud came out of the house with a bale-like bundle, which he threw into the back of the sleigh as he mounted. "Got to take our foot in our hand," he said only, and urged the horses to speed. "Might not make it at that."

They did not make it. The train was pulling out. "I'm right down sorry, Mr. Wilkerson," said Bertha faintly. "If'n it hadn't a-ben fer me—"

He patted her hand. "Now don't you think a thing about it, Mis' Mallory. It'll git off in the mornin'; don't make no differ'nce. Set still, set still. I'm a-goin' to take you home."

But Bertha demurred. "I want to walk," she said, and hurriedly dismounted. "I thank you kindly, Mr. Wilkerson."

She did not give him time to protest her decision, but plunged away doggedly through the piled-up snow. The sight of the "deepot," the sound of the vanishing train, nauseated her with the memory of the woman. It was hard to walk in such snow, it would take a long time, but she could not bear Bud's kindness any longer.

A gust of hatred for Tim shook her, body and mind. "I wisht he'd kill me, so they c'd hang him fer it," she thought grimly. "He won't, though. He ain't got the guts." She plodded on. "All he's good fer is beatin' up on helpless young 'uns and suckin' up to Brother Pointer at them there meetin's, actin' like he's sech a all-fired good Christian."

She resented Brother Pointer bitterly, too. "If'n it hadn't a-ben fer him I might 'a' got somewheres. Mr. Plant liked me. He kissed me, didn't he? But that there meddlesome old fool kep' a-hangin' around!''

The Mallory farm came in sight. There was no smoke rising. She supposed none of them had come back, even Clarence.

She stopped. Then where had he gone? Where was he now?

She began to run, half failing at every step. Her heart thudded against her ribs as though to break them. "Clance! Clance!" she gasped as she floundered, "wait a minute, Clance!" If she had only let Bud drive her home! "I'd 'a' ben there long ago," she panted. "Clance, you wait—"

But the house was empty and cold, the kitchen fire still banked. She flung open the damper as she passed and, throwing off coat and shawl, ran into the bedroom shared by the three boys. The curtain across the corner had been pulled aside. Clarence's Sunday clothes, the only ones he had besides overalls and hickory shirts and the cap and mackinaw he had been wearing, were gone.

Bertha's heart stopped. That train. That train at the station.

But would he have had any money?

He might have. He might have had Milltown dance money hidden away. Or he might have found money of Tim's and taken it. He might have been there on that very train at the station. He might have seen her come driving up with Bud.

It seemed to Bertha that her heart split then; split like the rind of a melon, with a tearing noise. But it did not bleed. There was no pain left in it now, there was nothing but fear.

She flew into the front room, stared at the wall. The fiddle was gone too.

She ran back into the kitchen, feeling dizzy, and came up sharply against the edge of the table, causing a dollop of cold suds to leap from the dishpan. She plunged her hands into the water and leaned forward on her palms, vaguely aware of the familiar shapes of eggbeater and butcher knife at the bottom of the pan. "Clance," she whispered. "He's went plumb off. I won't never see him no more."

Someone stamped on the snow outside the kitchen door. She knew that Tim was coming, and involuntarily her hand closed around the knife. She did not look at him as he opened the door. "Where's Clance at?" she asked him, hoping against hope.

" 'Where's Clance at?' " he mocked her. "Clance, Clance, Clance, Clance, Clance! Wouldn't you jest like to know where Clance is at?"

"Yes, I would," said Bertha steadily. "And if'n you know where he's at, Tim Mallory, you better tell me."

Tim cackled. "Whooptydoodledo! Look who's a-talkin'! Look who's a-wearin' the pants!" He threw off his windbreaker, tossed it on a chair and spat into the woodbox. "Why in time don't you put some wood on that there fire? You want the whole kit and bilin' to freeze to death?" He slammed the door open and thrust in a chunk or two. "I ain't got no idy whereabouts your doll-baby sugartit's at, and I don't keer. All I know is I'll tan the livin' hide offen him if he ain't here by—"

Bertha drew the knife out of the water. "No, you won't, Tim," she said levelly and softly. "No, you won't. You won't never git to tan nobody no more. You done tanned the livin' hide offen the last pore young 'un you're ever a-goin' to." She came toward him. He stared at her, his mouth falling open. "Put down that there knife! You goin' crazy, or what?"

He backed away, but Bertha came relentlessly on. She did not hurry. "I seen you that day you was out there in the medder," she told him, still in the calm tones of ordinary conversation, "that time you was a-beltin' the breath outen Clovis till he couldn't even cry, an' him a-gaggin' and a-wallerin' in the weeds like a cripple dog. Doc Brumbaugh, he seen him next day too, and so'd Brother Pointer. And Mr. Plant seen him when he went back to school and couldn't even stand up straight when he walked. You're a mighty big man around these here parts, Tim. Ever'body talks about what a big man you are." She made a sudden feint at him with the knife, and at his terror-stricken yelp she laughed aloud. "Why, Tim, you ain't skeered, are you? A great big man like you?"

Tim turned to run, but she was between him and the door before he could reach it. He started for the window; again she intercepted him. "Looks like you're right down skeered, Tim. How does it feel? How do you like bein' skeered outen your senses? You ben a-skeerin' young 'uns all your life, now how do you like it?"

Tim's breath rattled in his throat as he tried to speak. He did not look at the knife. It was Bertha's eyes that held him, and her hair, that blazed above her face like a nimbus of fire. "Y- y- you—" he gasped.

She moved a little nearer. "Git down and waller, Tim," she directed silkily. "Git down there on the floor and waller like Clovis. I want to see you wallerin', jest oncet." She lunged at him. "You hear me?"

Tim dropped. He found his voice, an agonized squeak. "Fer the love o' God, Berthy, don't do nothin' to me! Don't, for Christ's sake—" Her lip curled. "I thought so," she said with satisfaction. "I always knowed you wasn't nothin' but a miser'ble low-down, sneakin', bullyin', cowardly little piece o' nothin'. Jest a little biggety banty rooster a-callin' itself a man. Git all the way down there!" She brandished the knife again. "Git down on your worthless yeller belly and crawl. Crawl while you kin, Tim. Lemme see you crawl. You won't never git to stand up on two feet agin."

He groveled, yammering. "Fer God's sake, Berthy, don't do nothin' to me! I'll git Clance a fiddle—I'll let him go to town! Air you a woman or a devil? Put down that knife!"

She drove it, with all her strength, between his shoulder-blades, and his words died in a thick, bubbling gurgle. "Like a stuck pig," Bertha thought dispassionately. She watched his brief death struggle without emotion. When he was quite still she set her foot firmly against his body and, grasping the handle of the knife, pulled it out and tossed it back into the dishpan.

There was blood on her right hand and forearm. She

washed it off. Blood on the skirt of her dress too, but that did not matter.

She walked out of the kitchen and into the front room, sitting down in the rocker and pushing her hair from her forehead. She looked about her as if for something to do. But the house was clean, as always. Nothing called her.

She leaned back in the chair. "I feel right good," she thought. "Seems like maybe I kin git along somehow now."

Even the thought of Clarence did not disturb her. He would get along, too, a big strong boy like Clance. Mr. Plant had always said he would get along.

Mr. Plant! Bertha threw back her head and laughed aloud. "I must 'a' ben plumb outen my head," she thought. "Why, even Bud Wilkerson's bigger'n him, and better! *He* wasn't skeered to make over me and call me honey when he seen I was havin' trouble."

Mr. Plant had "made over" her, too. He had even kissed her; but Bertha knew now that it was not the same. She knew now why Bud's kindness had overwhelmed her. It was that he had given her what Jeff Plant could not. Could not and would not, because to him she was different.

She remembered thinking, one day long ago, "I don't reckon Mr. Plant'd look down on me." But he did. He had kissed her that day and told her she was "priceless." But would he have said that to that other woman?

He had said, "My God, Bertha, aren't we friends, you and I?" But they were not. If they had been, he wouldn't have spoken of Opal as though she didn't matter. "He only kissed me because he'd wrote a book. *She* wasn't there fer him to kiss, so he kissed me, that's all." She remembered his question, "You want I should send you a copy?" Why, that was mocking her, just as Tim mocked her. What difference?

Her sense of justice compelled her to make some distinction. "He never meant it mean, like Tim. He liked me all right. But he jest liked me the way you like a dog." She glanced down at her hands. "Buttermilk!" she scoffed, and then, on a sobering thought, "I'll miss them books."

From where she sat she could just see one of Tim's legs.

"He don't feel so biggety now," she thought with satisfaction. "I better do somethin' about him pretty soon."

But she could not command herself to action. "Seems like I jest want to keep on a-settin' here restin'. Seems like I ain't had a rest like this in years."

She thought of Opal and Hughie. "They ain't nothin' but babies; they ain't got no sense," she murmured indulgently. She thought of her other children, and a sweet pain stirred at her heart. She wished them within call, that she might take them in her arms and carry them back through time to their mother's breast. "I'll be good to 'em now," she promised. "I'll make up fer it all."

She had little doubt that she could, for she knew her strength. In the new clean peace that sang in her body like wine she knew, too, that she was not without aid or resource as she had imagined. The "notions" she needed would come to her now at call, just as they always had to Mr. Plant. He had given her that much, anyhow, with his books and his talk and the things he had said about teaching. " 'Twould 'a' made more sense," she thought regretfully, "if'n I'd 'a' listened to him more and not looked at him so much." For how did she know, after all, that Opal and Daisy and the twins and Ardeth had nothing in them to "git ahold of"? If Tim could knock out all power to think from her mind, what might he not have been able to do to the children? It was a miracle that even Clance had escaped him.

"Brother Pointer'd say that there God of his'n done it," she mused, and felt her heart suddenly pause. "He might be right, at that. You can't prove it he ain't."

New and strange and startling as the idea was, it did not baffle Bertha, to whom there was nothing even surprising, let alone baffling, in the possibility that God had agreed with her about Clarence. "I bet if I ast Him, He'd help with the rest of 'em, too. He knowed all the time I never had a lick o' sense; He ain't a-goin' to hold it aginst me now."

By "it" she meant her long neglect of her children, her imbecile infatuation with a stranger and her stubborn resistance to the overtures of Divinity as Brother Pointer had represented them to her. The killing of Tim did not enter in at all. She thought of it, but only fleetingly: "I ort to 'a' done it a long time ago. How do I know he ain't crippled them young 'uns so bad I can't never git 'em straightened out agin?"

But she did not believe it. There was plenty left within her to deal with the children, and if God was there—"and I b'lieve to my soul He is," Bertha thought, amazed—He would certainly help her. He'd have to. "What elst would He want with a ornery piece like me? Here He's run me down like Molly run down that there rabbit, or tried to, and it looks like He's catched me fer fair; and I ben mad at Him ever sence I c'n remember, and here I ain't mad at all. I feel right good about Him. Now ain't that funny?" She drew a long shivering breath. "But we've shore got us a job on our hands, I reckon."

This reminder, as always, brought her to her feet. Not even the intransigence of the Hound of Heaven, unknown and undreamed of till now, could stay old habit. She needed help now, human help; God would wait till she found it. There were things that had to be done. It would take her too long to manage by herself, even if she had known what she ought to do. Who was there she could ask? Bud Wilkerson was too far away, and so was the teacher, even if she had wanted him; and Clance was gone.

She crossed the room to the window, pulling the curtain aside. There was a man out there, plodding up the road through the half-trodden snow. Brother Pointer! Bertha's heart leaped up with pleasure and love at the sight. "I ben right ornery to him, and him so good," she thought with a rush of remorse.

She sped out into the yard as she was, without a wrap. "Brother Pointer! Brother Pointer!"

The old man halted and turned. Recognizing her, he lifted his cap in his usual kindly greeting. "Evenin', Mis' Mallory. Ain't you too cold out here without no coat?" He crossed through a drift of snow to the fence to meet her. "Ain't nothin' the matter, is they?"

Bertha came up to the fence, panting. She was smiling, and she could see that this surprised him. "I ain't cold," she said, "but I need some help, Brother Pointer. Tim's dead in there. I killed him."

Brother Pointer's jaw dropped. "Mis' Mallory! You never—" He caught sight of the blood on her skirt and set his hand on the top rail of the fence to steady himself. "Berthy, you ain't—you never—you don't mean to tell me—you couldn't—"

She nodded. "Anybody could. It 'uz easy. That there old dull beat-up butcher knife jest went plumb through him like he was a rotten piece o' cheese."

She smiled, and at Brother Pointer's horrified face was overcome with compassion. She leaned forward, putting her hand warmly over his mittened one on the fence. Her face was illumined like a loving child's. "Why, Brother Pointer," she exclaimed, "you're so cold you're a-shakin' all over! You come in a minute. I got a nice fire in the kitchen. I'd like right well to make you a hot cup o' coffee."

The trembling old man stared at her, still agape. Bertha met his gaze frankly, beaming. "Besides," she added, after a long deep breath, "I need to talk to you, Brother Pointer. I want you should tell me what I better do."